FAERY NOVICE

THE FAERY CHRONICLES BOOK ONE

LESLIE CLAIRE WALKER

sfp

FAERY NOVICE

~

When Kevin's ten-point plan for a normal life meets the magic of Faery, he discovers what courage really means.

A Halloween party turns unhinged when Kevin begins to hear other people's thoughts. The last thing he wants to be is different, but he can't shut out this magic. He can't deny the secret world of the Faery underground. Or the girl who tempts his imagination and his heart.

His rising power drives him into her world and threatens to turn the Faery underground upside down, drawing him into an epic battle with Faery King.

Kevin's chosen family, including the powerful witch Stacy, rallies behind him. But he must be brave and strong enough to triumph or risk losing them all...

CHAPTER 1

METAL THUNDERED over the sound system so hard it shook the dust off the backyard lawn furniture. Half the junior and senior classes had cups of trashcan punch in their hands and the other half crammed themselves into the pool and the hot tub until they were filled with more bodies than water. I swayed, standing at the water's edge, early on my way to buzzed.

And on my way to scoring with the one girl I'd wanted to kiss all year, Amy Mathis. She of the long, blue-black hair that reminded me of crow's feathers. She of the chipped black nail polish and the black pants with the homemade chains that hung halfway down her ass. The tank top that hugged every curve—and those were some luscious curves.

I had to yell to lift my voice over the music. "What are you doing tomorrow?"

She sipped her punch and shook her head. "What?"

I leaned to whisper in her ear and caught her scent. Something with vanilla. And leather.

I breathed her in, could've done just that—only that—for an hour. But I *would not* do something that utterly creepy, no matter how tempted. No matter how fuzzed my mind felt. I wanted her to go out with me. I wanted her to feel safe with me.

"Tomorrow," I said. "Movie?"

She moved closer. "Can't tomorrow. I have a family thing."

I cocked my head so I could see her eyes, trying to tell if she was making excuses, letting me down easy. A clue I would've been able to get easier if I hadn't already dipped my brain in a vat of hundred-proof liquid.

Her eyes were deep green, like jade, and honest. So I could ask for a rain check without making an ass of myself. I tried not to let her see my relief. "Friday?"

"Halloween?" The corner of her mouth quirked into a half-smile. "It's a date, Kev—"

She never finished saying my name—but shoved into me, her drink flooding the front of my shirt.

I rocked back on my heels, unable to hold my footing, and tumbled into the pool, with Amy on top of me.

We sank to the bottom, five-and-a-half-feet down. The chill of the water soaked in and rose all the skin on my body to gooseflesh and shrank my balls down to raisins. The taste of chlorine filled my nose and mouth and stung my eyes. Amy's hair floated around us like feathers.

I twined my fingers with hers and squeezed, pushing off the bottom for both of us, sputtering to the surface and helping Amy to the edge. She held onto the concrete and coughed her lungs out.

"Sorry," someone said.

I looked up at the someone. Rude Davies. Short for Rudolph Diamond Davies III, six-three, two-fifty, with buzz-cut orange hair and a red Hawaiian shirt, whose house this was. And whose parents were conveniently in Colorado for the weekend.

"Sorry," Rude said again. He held out a hand.

He was serious with the apology. Nickname aside, Rude was a good guy. Besides, if he meant to push us into the pool, we'd have known it was coming. One thing Rude couldn't do to save his life? Sneak up on anybody.

"That's okay, man. But payback is hell."

The big guy grinned and lifted Amy, and then me, out of the water.

The air may have been toastier than usual for late October, but that didn't translate to warm enough to stand in while soaking wet. The wind gusted, shocking me completely sober.

"Y'all are freezing," Rude said.

Amy hugged herself. "Talk to me about the pool in July."

That went for me, too. Except for the part where the pool had done wonders for Amy's tank top. I tried not to stare—or not too hard, anyway. "You need a towel."

"Me? You mean *we*." She laughed. "Drowned rat's the new pink."

I really did like this girl. And it looked mutual. "Wait here. I'll scare us up some."

I didn't have too much trouble elbowing a path to the house since no one wanted to get wet by association. Except one girl who didn't get out of my way fast enough. Long, curly blond hair, eyebrow ring.

Hazel eyes betraying no alcoholic influence, she smiled at me. Not a nervous reflex. A real grin. Weird, and so much so that I kept an eye on her as she disappeared into the crowd.

On that trajectory, I caught sight of my best friend, Scott, whom I'd come to the party with, imbibing yet another cup of punch. His long blond hair hung in his face, but couldn't hide his huge grin and glassy eyes.

How many drinks did that make? Five? Six? A little out of hand.

Scott raised his glass. "A toast, Kevin!"

Embarrassing—couldn't say for Scott, but being the target of his drunken joy made my ears burn and my skin flush five shades of red. I ducked inside the house. Ten steps down the long hall, linen closet at the end, across from the bathroom. I opened the door and pulled out two of the richest towels I'd ever seen. Who had towels this thick?

Rude did. He also had someone to wash and fold them and clean the house and a whole lot of other things I'd never see in this lifetime. For a good, long second, I felt jealous, but I didn't like the thoughts that started to worm their way into my head. Stuff like whether Rude deserved to have so much. Why some guys got so lucky, and other guys ended up taking care of the house and the grocery shopping while their dads spent evenings guzzling beer and watching Sports Center as the finances got tighter.

Shut up, Kev.

It wasn't like Rude's life was perfect, either. More perfect, yeah, but only in the got-money department. Rude's parents expected him to be the next President of the United States. The pressure to get the grades, to run for school office, to stay on everyone's good side? It was too much. Which was probably why Rude's greatest ambition was to see his picture in the senior yearbook on the page under LIFE OF THE PARTY.

This party sucks out loud.

I heard the words loud and slurred and close, as if someone next to me had yelled.

Except no one had. I was alone in the hall. I must've hallucinated. I pushed it firmly out of mind. I'd head back to Amy. Be a towel-carrying hero.

I think I'm cool to drive.

More words from no one and nowhere. What the hell?

I blinked. It seemed as if I hadn't heard the words with my ears—I'd heard them in my mind. It made no sense. I was having an excellent time, nowhere near wanting to leave. No way would I have thought for two seconds about driving.

I stood there holding the towels for half a minute, waiting to see if it would happen again. And annoyed as hell. I had Amy to get back to. I didn't want to lose her to some other guy who happened to be there and more convenient.

I shut the closet door and started back down the hall to outside, where my dripping-wet, might-be-girlfriend waited. One step, two steps, three. Then I heard:

Keys.

Dammitall to hell.

I looked around. Had somebody slipped something into my punch? Had being pushed into the pool made me lose my mind?

Puh-lease. Someone had to be playing tricks on me. Someone

familiar, by the sound and tone of the voice. Scott, maybe. The voice sounded a lot like Scott.

I waited for my buddy to do it again. I mentally *dared* him to do it again. When I didn't hear anything else weird, I slowly started to relax.

I shook my head. Chalked the whole thing up to the punch and the party vibe. I wouldn't even remember it in the morning. Which, if I got lucky, wouldn't come for a very long time. I could have hours with Amy.

I kept my eyes front and center, and walked down that hall like I owned it. Until I emerged into the living room. It took me a crazy minute to compute what I saw.

Scott. Looking for his keys. In the entry hall. Where the key sergeant guarded the bowl so no one could drive home tanked. Except the key sergeant was nowhere in sight.

Scott focused like his life depended on it, digging into the mass of metal and plastic and leather. His fingers closed around the right set of keys—the ones that went with Scott's father's Mustang, with the silver horse keychain.

Scott closed his eyes. His voice—no doubt in my mind that it was his—invaded my brain again.

I'm think I'm gonna blow.

I heard that so strong, I felt the nausea, too. My knees wobbled. I dropped the towels.

But Scott didn't throw up. He pulled himself together and headed for the front door.

"Hey!" I yelled after him.

But Scott sped out the door like a bullet.

I followed, only half-aware of shoving people out of the way. I tripped over the threshold and into the yard just in time to see the Mustang's lights flash twice where Scott had parked it at the curb.

"Wait!" I yelled again.

But Scott either didn't hear, or he didn't want to. He slid into the driver's seat and started the engine.

Which left me only one choice.

I stepped into the street. Into the path of the car.

CHAPTER 2

S COTT HIT THE GAS—and spotted me a second too late to stop in time.

I heard him think *OH SHIT* before he stomped on the brake.

I backpedaled as fast as I could. The bumper still nicked my leg, knocking me off balance. No water to cushion the fall this time—I hit the asphalt hard enough to lose all the air in my lungs. The street and the car and the cracked curb and the grass beyond it blurred. For a second, I thought I'd pass out, but then the world rushed back into sharp focus.

Footsteps vibrated the pavement—people running—and a car door opened.

Scott hunkered down next to me. He reeked of beer, at least in part because he'd spilled some on his skull-and-crossbones T-shirt. And on his leather boots, the sticky, steel toes of which menaced an inch from my head.

The pupils of Scott's coal-black eyes were dilated, his lips curled in a snarl. He looked Godzilla-sized, but that had to be the angle and the alcohol, because he was my size, maybe a little smaller.

He clutched the car keys in his fist and boy, did he look pissed.

Angry? Oh, yeah. Scott wanted to hit me.

"Are you fucking crazy, Kevin?" he spat.

"I should ask you that." I got my elbows under me and pushed up. I expected to be dizzy, but no. I lobster-crawled back a couple of feet and stood up slowly. "You can't drive, man. You didn't check out with the sergeant."

"What was I supposed to do, hunt him down?"

"Those are the rules."

Scott rose and moved in, nose-to-nose. "You saying I'm drunk?"

"I am."

An actual crowd had formed around us. Folks from the yard, from inside the house. And from poolside: Rude elbowed his way to the front. Amy pushed her way in behind him. And behind her, the blond with a silver ring in her eyebrow, the one I recognized but didn't know.

Rude took in the whole scene in a heartbeat. He glared at Scott. "What do you think you're doing?" He held out his hand, palm-up. "Hand 'em over, dude."

Scott shook his head. "What're you gonna do? Make me?"

"Yeah," Rude said. Plain as that. Do what he said or get squashed.

Against all logic, Scott turned back toward the car. Rude grabbed him by the arm. Scott took a swing, proving my point—because sober, he'd never have been dumb enough to try something like that.

Rude not only blocked the shot, he leveled Scott with a right hook to the jaw. Rude scooped up the keys to the 'stang, then handed them to Amy. "Park that thing, will you?"

She slid into the driver's seat.

A female voice slid into my head. *Damn kids damn kids damn kids. I'll show them.*

Definitely not Amy's voice.

I scanned the yard as the crowd headed back inside, and something off to the side caught my eye. Nosy neighbor lady next door, peeking through her curtains.

She scowled at me. *Little asshole.*

I was *not* little.

That woman was going to call the cops. I knew it like I knew my own name. I opened my mouth to tell Rude, but he'd already gone back inside.

The nearest police station was ten minutes away, max.

I looked over at Amy again. She turned the key in Scott's ignition. The engine hummed. *Let's go,* she mouthed.

I heard the words in my mind at the same time I read them on her lips.

She'd seen what I had and come to the same conclusion about the neighbor. I wished that made me feel less suddenly crazy. I wished I had time to wonder what the hell was going on.

"Wait," I said. I hoped to hell she would.

I hurried inside and found Rude in the living room. The big guy loomed over Scott, who was laid out on the sofa, half-conscious.

Rude glanced over his shoulder. "He's coming around."

"Good," I said. "The cops are coming."

"You hear sirens?" Rude asked.

I shook my head. "I just know."

I couldn't tell him how. He didn't ask.

"Thanks, dude." He headed out back to start rounding people up.

I eyed Scott. He'd done the stupid thing, but I didn't want him to go to jail. I hauled his dead weight off the sofa with a grunt.

"What?" he mumbled.

"Carrying your dazed ass out of here. Just shut it and walk if you can."

He could, just enough so I didn't have to lift him anymore. Still, it was slow going. Slower than I wanted.

By the time we wove our way through tipped-off party people already screaming out the door and landed on the driveway, sirens wailed. By the sound of them, the police were only a few streets over and closing in by the second.

Everyone who'd been at the party piled into their rides and took off—or they couldn't get out because others blocked them in.

Amy and the Mustang should've been snarled in the mess. But they'd disappeared. She'd left.

I maneuvered Scott onto the sidewalk and kept moving. If we

could get far enough away before the real trouble went down, maybe we'd be okay. Before I could think too much more about our choices —run on foot (which was definitely not happening) or hide—something flashed red four houses down, taillights on a black car in the halo of a streetlamp. Amy's head poked out of the top. Out of the sunroof.

I aimed for Amy and pushed hard. "Move it, man. Gotta go, pronto."

The cops were so close that by the time we tumbled into the car and Amy put the pedal to the metal, I could hear the police think—had to be them, or else I was losing my damn mind.

I slapped my hands over my ears. Didn't help at all.

I got a mindful of thoughts about how rich kids never think they're gonna get caught breaking the law and how the cops expected to make at least twenty arrests. How "these kids" would be in deep shit with their parents.

The last thing I heard before Amy turned the corner freaked me even worse.

The cops weren't just coming to shut down the party. They were there to look for me.

CHAPTER 3

I TRIED NOT TO PANIC—or at least not to show it. I met Amy's gaze. "Jam. *Now.*"

She got the message. She put some blocks behind us. We didn't say another word until we'd gone a mile in the dark and quiet without picking up a blue-and-white tail.

She sighed about the same time I let myself think about relaxing.

"You got problems I don't know about?" she asked.

"All kinds."

"Like?"

I sneaked out of the house at night to party, but mostly just to get some space. I'd skipped out on my tab last weekend at Hooligans, though I'd made it into the club in the first place with a fake ID, so if the bartender remembered a name, at least it wouldn't be mine. Minor transgressions. None of it bad enough to come back to haunt me like this.

I was the proverbial Good Kid. I had all As, one B, and my teachers liked me. I could get away with a lot more than I tried to, but I wanted to go away to college and I'd have to do it on a scholarship. Have to be a full ride, because money was scarcer than water in the desert. I needed to be far away.

Somewhere I wouldn't feel like prisoner.

Amy raised a brow.

I was supposed to say something, wasn't I? "Don't worry about it. We escaped. It's still early. We've got wheels."

"True. But your friend looks like shit."

I glanced back at Scott, who'd passed out in the back seat. He'd be pissed when he woke up, and probably not at Rude. Honestly, Rude couldn't have done anything except what he did. Rules were rules. No, Scott would be mad at me. His best friend. The guy who hadn't trusted him, who'd ratted him out. Maybe he'd have made it home, or wherever else he'd been headed, with no problem.

Or maybe he'd have wrecked himself or someone else. I knew what that was like. I knew it close to the bone.

My dad had smashed us up once, and once was more than enough for a lifetime. And then there'd been the accident (let's call it what it was—vehicular homicide) that'd stolen my mom's life.

She'd been hit head-on by a guy who'd left a bar after having ten too many. It hadn't even been a year. Halloween night would be the anniversary of the four-in-the-morning ring of the doorbell, when the police had come to give us the bad news.

I refused to go any further with that thought. I would. Not. Think. About. Her.

If anyone should be mad here, it ought to be me. If anyone should've thrown that punch at Scott, it should've been me.

I took a deep breath, pretending not to notice how shaky it felt. "Scott's gonna have a helluva bruised-up face tomorrow. And a headache aspirin won't touch."

But he'd be alive.

"We should take him home now," I said.

She nodded. "I wish tonight had turned out different."

"We could've hung out at Rude's a lot longer."

"Nah. We could've gone someplace else."

"Where?"

"Anywhere," she said.

Anywhere as long as it was private. Tonight could've turned out way different. I sighed. "We still good for Friday?"

"We are." Her lips curved in her quirky half-grin.

That one smile could hold me all week. That and my imagination.

She drove to her place, five minutes away through side streets lined with small, brick houses, most of them with the drapes shut or the blinds closed. Pines, magnolias, and oaks in the front yards, some with limbs shading the street.

Amy's house was dark except for the blazing porch light. She swung the car into the drive, the Mustang's headlights sweeping across flowerbeds full of lilies and monkey grass, disturbing a black cat with yellow eyes that loped across the drive into the neighbor's property.

From where Amy parked, I could see a set of white-painted wooden rockers and a side table with a glass half-full of dark liquid that might've been iced tea. Above the seats, a copper wheel hung from the eaves, twirling in the breeze.

We got out of the car, and I hugged her goodbye. I liked the way she felt this close to me.

"Friday," she said, her breath warming my neck.

"Can't wait."

I watched her walk up and go in. Then I settled in the driver's seat, her vanilla and leather scent clinging to me. I closed my eyes and breathed it in deep.

Something touched my shoulder. I jumped half a foot off of the seat.

"Where the hell are we?" Scott asked. "Why are you driving? And why am I back here?"

Unbelievable. "Aren't you supposed to be passed out, genius?"

Scott shook his head, very carefully. After a second, he said, "Rude hits like a girl. It was Rude who put me on my ass, wasn't it?"

I laughed. "There's girls that could kick your ass from here to the moon."

He blinked at me. "But it was Rude?"

I laughed. "You want to ride shotgun?"

He mulled the thought. "Not wise to move too much, man."

"You gotta boot, tell me and I'll pull over."

It took twenty minutes to take Scott home and get him in the house without waking up his parents. Neither of us was exactly graceful, so I considered it a minor miracle.

Almost immediately, the adrenaline drained out of my body, leaving me plain exhausted. Smart thing to do was to call my dad, explain the sitch, and stay the rest of the night at Scott's. But I just wanted to go home. Sleep in my own bed, wake up in the morning, and forget about everything, hoping not to have nightmares about what might've happened.

I especially wanted to forget I'd ever heard anyone's thoughts. Because that was crazy, and I was the sanest guy I knew.

I headed out on foot. The night settled around me, the air cool against my skin, the silence of the streets and houses taking up residence in my head. A breeze soft as a caress stirred the leaves on the trees to a whisper.

The world felt fragile.

Two blocks down the line, in sight of my house, I understood why. And I felt like a dumbass for not having thought more about those cops back at Rude's and what they'd wanted with me.

A police car crouched in my driveway, behind my dad's dirty Suburban.

I ducked and ran across the street, taking cover behind the Brown-backers' rosemary hedge, outside the circle of bright halogens under their eaves.

Rosemary for remembrance, Mom used to say.

Ten minutes later—every second of them an eternity—the cops meandered out of the house. Both of them were guys. One stocky Latino with watchful eyes and a gold pinky ring, and one redheaded, freckled, beer-gutted white dude. Funny—they didn't bounce right away. They hung around the car and casual-like scanned the street.

Pinky Ring's gaze passed over the spot where I hid. The hair on the back of my neck stood up like antennae, and nausea hit me like a gut punch.

I'd been pulled over for speeding and I'd been scrutinized going into clubs and nothing like this had ever happened before. The cop had done something to me. I didn't know what. I didn't want to know.

How was something like that even possible?

I braced my hands in the grass, solid and steady. Waited for the cop to look my way again. To catch sight of me. Call me out.

I could run if I had to.

And even as the thought crossed my mind, I knew how stupid that would be.

But the officer moved on, checking out the next-door neighbors' yards. He and the redhead looked at each other, shrugged, and got in the car.

They drove away. I watched until their taillights faded into the night and then had another dumbass thought.

No way those two were really cops.

CHAPTER 4

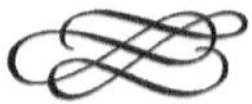

M Y DAD, FRANK, OPENED THE DOOR before I had a chance to dig my keys out of my pocket.

He was six-one and wiry, still in the light blue button-down shirt he'd worn to his job as an accounts payable clerk at a law firm, sleeves rolled up and the muscles corded in his forearms. He pushed his dark hair out of his eyes, one strand sticking up because of a cowlick. All the normal worry lines etched deep into his face. And he was seriously pissed.

Judging by the exaggerated way he clenched and unclenched his fists, I gauged Tonight's Beer Consumption at five.

He stepped out of the way, giving me space to come in, to see the muted TV running police procedural reruns, to hear the computer chirp.

The screen showed a picture of a bunch of guys riding horses through the air in formation like a flock of geese, along with a bunch of search results for something called the Wild Hunt, whatever that was. Sometimes Dad looked at unusual stuff online. But this? Not porn or politics. *Folklore.*

How weird was that?

Dad shut and locked the door behind us so quietly, I could hear the tumblers click home.

When he turned around, he met my gaze. "I'm only going to ask you this once, Kev. Did you know a girl was killed at your friend's house tonight?"

"What?" I'd known or recognized all the people at that party. "Who was she? What happened?"

"The cops wouldn't tell me much, Kevin. You did see the cops in here, didn't you?"

I stared. "Yeah."

"She was in her twenties, they said. Too old for all of you."

Someone I didn't know after all. Thank God. But she was still dead and—

"You were at the party with this girl?"

"I was with Scott. At Rude's."

"Uh-huh." He sighed. "How the hell do you end up in these situations? No—what I want to know is why, Kev. Why?"

That was unfair. And what did he mean by "these situations"? I didn't have an answer that wouldn't be snark.

I'm a bad seed. I'm the black sheep. Or the best reason, *Because I can.*

"I don't know, Dad."

"Oh, I think you do."

"I just want to be with my friends."

"Peer pressure."

"Sure, whatever."

"I taught you better than that. Your mother taught you better than that."

The ace card in his Deck of Guilt, played so soon. Bringing up Mom was fighting dirty. I shut off the feelings that threatened to well up. Somebody had to be logical here. Someone had to be in control.

"You're grounded," his father said. "Two weeks."

"Two weeks?"

"You were at an illegal party. A girl died. Police came to the house."

"I have a date Friday night."

"Cancel the date."

The hell I would.

Dad held up a hand to cut me off. "You'll cancel it, or it'll be three weeks."

I bit my tongue to keep from making things worse. As far as Dad was concerned, his word was the law around here.

But as far as I was concerned, he couldn't keep me in this house. I would *not* miss the date with Amy.

I said the only words Dad would tolerate right now. "Yes, sir."

"You go to school, you come straight home. Dinner had better be on the table when I get here. You do the dishes when we're through eating. You go to your room and do your homework. No Internet unless it's school-related. Wake up in the morning and do it all over again. Understood?"

My blood began to boil, heat building in my belly and rising toward my chest. "Yes, sir."

"Good." He folded his arms across his chest. "Your friend Rude—doesn't he have another name? A given name?"

"Yeah, he does."

I turned on my heel and stalked to my room.

I'd gone to a party where a girl had died, and I felt nauseated just thinking about who she was, who loved her and would miss her forever. But I also hadn't seen her, and no one else had, either.

Plus, what was with the cops—coming after me *before* they'd even got to the party? Before they'd found her?

What the hell had happened tonight?

I texted Rude, desperate for an answer—and fell asleep just before dawn, still waiting.

CHAPTER 5

SUNDAY: THE SILENT TREATMENT. Dad spent most of the day in his room, TV blaring consecutive football games. He came out once to point at the terminal mess that was my room. And I took that as my cue to smooth the rumpled sheets, to haul the pile of dirty laundry from the floor at the foot of the bed into the hamper in the closet. To spray some air freshener to cut the stink of dirty socks that hovered in the air like a storm cloud.

Nothing else to do, really. No knickknacks to shake the dust off of, unless you counted the six-pack of Coke tucked into the corner of my bookshelf. No framed pictures needing their glass shined. The lone poster on the wall? Wolverine had been there since I was, like, ten. The mutant could take care of himself.

After that, all I had was the essay due Tuesday afternoon for English—not that I could concentrate on it. It was hard to analyze Beowulf's battle with Grendel, with particular attention to Grendel's outcast status, with all the TV noise bleeding down the hall. Time for headphones. And blessed relief.

Also, I couldn't help but wonder what Dad was thinking, and on top of that be extra glad that I didn't hear those thoughts inside my head.

Clearly, last night I'd lost my mind. Had some kind of psychotic break at the party. Or maybe a psychic break.

Except I didn't believe in that kind of stuff. The psychic hotline on late-night TV, the shows about ghost hunters, the curandera with the storefront over on Westpark with the signs in the window about palm readings? Bunch of unprovable crap.

Problem was, I also didn't believe that ignoring things made them magically go away. I just didn't know what to do. Besides homework. And sleep.

The Monday morning alarm rang way too soon. Dad had already been up, made toast (judging by the dirty dishes in the sink), and headed out for work early. That had never happened before.

And it left me with a walk to school, which would take longer than I'd planned. I booked out the door with a breakfast bar in hand, hoping I hadn't forgotten anything.

I barely made it to homeroom before the bell. Amy smiled at me from her desk across the room when I walked in, and that was something. It made up for a lot.

She wore a patchwork hoodie she'd made herself. It hugged her body rather than camouflaging it. And it was unique, like she was.

We had first period Probability/Statistics together. She walked with me—by no means a small victory. The sexy scent of her perfume, the way she leaned in to me on the way to class, the warmth radiating from her skin—made me feel good.

And nervous in a way not helped by the fact that her girlfriends followed just out of earshot. What were their names? Oh, yeah. Britt-Don't-Call-Me-Brittany and Zoe.

"They talking about us?" I asked.

Amy mocked me with her eyes. "Why would they? Get over yourself, Kev."

"But I'm a brilliant, movie-star, athletic god."

Her mouth quirked into her special half-smile. "All right, yeah. They're talking about us. And also about you, but not about how brilliant you are."

"They already hate me?"

"They heard what happened after you left the party." Amy's grin faded.

I tensed even more. "What'd they hear?"

"That you knew the dead girl at the party. That you're a suspect."

"No. And no. Was there really a girl who died at Rude's house? I mean, how many people were there? Did anyone we know actually see her?"

She cocked her head at me as if to say, *If the cops said there was, then it happened.*

The whole situation was so wrong, I couldn't come up with a word for how wrong it was. "That look on your face—what's it about?"

"The cops came by my house yesterday. I told them you were with me at the party. Never left my side."

"Not exactly true."

"Close enough for government work. Whatever that means. Anyway, I believe you, Kevin."

I shoved my hands into my pockets. The cops who'd come to the house Saturday night hadn't asked my dad to bring me in for an interview. They hadn't called. They hadn't showed again.

But they'd harassed Amy.

The cops who were supposedly after me. The cops who weren't cops.

"Thanks," I said.

She sidled closer to me as we walked. Mrs. V's room, coming up fast on the right. One hour of super-hard math, half of which I couldn't understand to save my life, coming right up. Amy squeezed my hand before she went to her seat at the desk in front of mine. A heartbeat later, the bell rang.

"Phones off," Mrs. V said sharply, and jumped straight into the lesson.

I focused on Amy to get through it, hoping she'd help me with the homework. Not only did she have the beauty, she had serious Brain Power.

Not like Britt and Zoe, each of them a whispering, mean-eyed mass of curly black hair and cutting looks when Mrs. V turned her back.

They stared at me like I was some kind of freak.

CHAPTER 6

SECOND PERIOD WAS NO BETTER than first. I tried to concentrate, to pay attention. But instead of taking in Chemistry factoids, I kept thinking I heard soft voices in the halls, all of them containing some telephone-game version of my nighttime visit with the police. How people knew that was a mystery. But they glanced at me when they thought I couldn't see. My hackles stood at attention.

Mr. Nance, the school counselor, stopped me in the hall after class. Actually, it was more like I almost ran him down by looking everywhere except where I was going, trying not to pay attention to the voices echoing against the tiled floors and walls and gray metal lockers, trying to move fast and make myself small. Invisible.

I caught sight of the guy's shined brown dress shoes just in time to avoid bowling him over. He actually had on a suit, brown like the shoes, with pinstripes, no tie. He wore his salt-and-pepper hair slicked back, though a couple of strands fell across his face on account of the near-impact.

I'd only been to see the man once before. He'd helped me with college applications and scholarships. He'd been all business then and generally hard to read. Still, I'd gotten the impression that the guy understood how important that scholarship money was to me, and he hadn't judged. That was unusual and therefore cool.

"I'm sorry to hear about the events of the weekend," Nance said.

"Why would you say that?" Not that Nance's mysterious knowing would be any different than anybody else's, but to stop in the middle of the hall and talk about it? Very not cool.

"Isn't it better to have something said to your face?" the counselor asked.

The question made me scratch my head. By the time I understood that maybe Nance had done me some kind of weird favor, the counselor had given me a *cat got your tongue?* look and walked off. Which made me feel dumb.

And if I thought that was bad, lunch sucked worse.

I'd made it through the line to pick up my free meal (tomato-sauce-drowned meatloaf-looking thing, mashed potatoes with lumpy gravy, the ubiquitous green beans of doom) and barely sat down in my usual seat when Scott filled the space across the table from me, plunking down his tray so hard his milk spilled over the side of the carton. His left eye was a rainbow of painful black and purple, his cheeks were puffed out and ready to burst like he had something to say and had held onto it until now.

He went heavy on the sarcasm. "Thanks a lot, Kev."

"I had to stop you, man."

Scott settled down in his chair and shoveled beans into his mouth. "I'm not talking about that. Christ."

"Then what are you talking about?"

"The detectives who came to your house. They came to mine, too. Asked me a bunch of stuff I couldn't answer without getting in deep with my dad, so I didn't. You know what they did?"

I could guess.

"They told my dad where I was Saturday night. How much I had to drink. That I was wasted. I'm so screwed."

No shit. Scott's dad should've been a Marine. He kept Scott on such a tight leash, the guy couldn't go out anywhere without lying about where he went and who he went with. Scott's dad had always been that way as far back as I remembered, since kindergarten.

"How long are you grounded for?"

"None of your business," Scott said.

I winced. "No, really."

"Really, man. I'm not supposed to hang out with you anymore. Dad's orders. If he finds out I—what'd he call it?—disrespected him again, I'm on a plane down to Harlingen, pronto."

"Military school?" Damn. The man had never threatened that before.

Scott finished with his beans and moved on to the potatoes. "So you get why I won't be around much from now on."

"You're actually gonna do what he tells you?" Even though Scott had spent years working around the rules, he hadn't been caught once. This time had been an aberration.

"The look on his face when he said it? Man, you should've been there," Scott said. "In fact, it should've been your ass on the hot seat."

"Right. Because it's all my fault."

"That's how I see it," Scott said.

"Your eyes are broken."

"So're you. You hear what everyone's saying?"

"You one of the people saying it?"

Scott didn't answer.

"You'd talk behind my back, but you won't say it to me?"

"I just did." Scott went to work on his mystery meatloaf with gusto. Like none of this bothered him at all. Like it didn't matter. He'd gone from being my friend to a betraying asshole in ten minutes.

"If that's how you feel, why're you sitting here?"

"I had to eat somewhere," Scott said. "Besides, I thought you deserved a heads-up."

From the guy who claimed to be my best friend. "Wow. Magnanimous, man."

"Don't let it go to your head," Scott said. He scraped his tray clean and vacated the spot before he'd even swallowed.

I got up immediately and headed out back. No desire to bask in the humiliation.

Rude caught up with me out there. The big guy pushed a newspaper into my hand and walked off, leaning against the brick wall over by the skater's island in the yard, where the rule was no smoking but he did anyway.

In fact, he looked conspicuous as hell in today's bright blue Hawaiian shirt. And yet no one called him on the cigarette he tapped out of the pack he kept in his shirt pocket or the cloud of smoke he blew into the wind. Security had special blind spots when it came to him.

I glanced down at the paper, which turned out to be the front page of the *Houston Chronicle*. Rude had highlighted an article below the fold.

WOMAN FOUND DEAD IN SOUTHWEST HOUSTON

An unidentified woman was found dead shortly after 2:00 AM in a bedroom at a home in Bellaire. The medical examiner confirms the cause of death as strangulation.

A spokesman said the police have several leads.

Aw, hell.

I walked over to where Rude stood. "Hey."

"Hey, yourself." Rude took a drag, turned his head to the side, and exhaled a stream of smoke.

"You didn't answer my text."

"Sorry, dude. No time. The police called my parents up at Angel Fire. They hopped the first flight out of Denver. I cleaned up the house before they got there, not that it mattered."

"Shit."

"My thoughts exactly," Rude said. "I keyed Mrs. Zephyr's car."

"Who?"

"The neighbor who ratted us out. She deserved it. She even had it out with my dad about it, but he didn't have too much patience with her. He didn't know something like that would happen and she ought to keep her car in the garage, what happened was her own lookout, not his. Blah, blah, blah." Rude dragged on his smoke.

"Did you know the girl?" I asked.

Who was she? Why didn't I see her? How could I not know?

Rude shook his head. "There was no girl."

I stared at him. "The fuck?"

"People in their twenties crash high school parties all the time, right? You know I never saw her body? Just the body bag the coroner carried out. And my folks—they went down to the station and came back kind of fuzzy about the whole thing."

A chill skittered up my spine.

"Listen, dude—I was watching those cops while they were at the house, too—the way they acted, what they assumed, the way they tried to steer the conversation. They've got a hard-on for you."

I didn't understand it. I didn't even know where to start. "I don't know why."

"They're not cops."

It was all I could do not to scream. I spoke through gritted teeth. "Explain it to me like I'm five."

"The whole thing stinks of magic."

"Magic. Like pulling rabbits out of hats?"

"No, dude. A spell."

Like witches? Or like hearing other people's thoughts? "You're joking."

"Do I look like I'm joking?"

He looked deadly serious. "Why would someone do that to me?"

"No idea yet. But they really wanted to ruin your life."

"It's working."

He nodded. "Look, I know a guy."

"What kind of guy?"

"The kind you pay to get the 411."

I got a sick feeling in the pit of my belly—the same sick feeling I always got when I had to explain that I couldn't afford something that other people took for granted. "Rude, I can't."

"No cash worries."

I raised a brow. I didn't want to be in debt to Rude or anyone else. I wanted to tell him no. But I had a very bad feeling I needed this help.

"I can pay you back, man," I said.

"No, really, Kev. He doesn't charge money."

Then how good could he be? *You get what you pay for* was a cliché for a reason. Still, the guy had to be better than nothing. "When do I meet him?"

"After school work for you?"

Except for the part where I needed to get home in enough time to cook dinner, before Dad got home from work. Then again, how long could the meeting take?

"It's good." Almost too good to be true, after what had happened with Scott. "Didn't your parents warn you away from me, too?"

"Yeah. Never do what I'm told, though."

I tried not to let my relief show.

Rude sucked his cigarette down to the filter and pitched it onto the grass, grinding the cherry out with his toe. "Just meet me back here later."

"Will do."

Rude plucked the butt off the ground and tucked it into an empty Altoids tin. "Leave no trace, man."

Keep it on the low. No problem. If there was anything I could keep, it was a secret.

I headed to gym, which today unfortunately meant a physical fitness test, complete with my arch-nemesis: pull-ups. What kind of teacher made a kid with skinny arms do that kind of thing? A sadist, that was who.

Well, at least I'd make up for it running the track. I could do that just about forever, and I didn't suck at it.

On the way, I realized I hadn't heard a single thought besides my own today. As fast as that craziness had started, it had ended. I hoped.

I was, of course, totally wrong.

CHAPTER 7

WE DROVE DEEP into west Houston in Rude's Explorer, vintage Metallica blaring from the speakers. I expected the car to stink of cigarette smoke and the ghost of cheeseburgers eaten on the fly, but it smelled brand new. I expected Rude to speed or run stoplights—to break the rules just like he did everywhere else—but he drove like my dad. It was unexpected.

The street signs went from the ones I was used to seeing, in English, to both English and Chinese. Mega-churches sidled up alongside mom-and-pop businesses with homemade signs I couldn't read. This close to rush hour, the roads began to crowd with traffic and the air filled with exhaust fumes and the smell of meat and spices. Restaurants prepping for the dinner rush.

All the way there, Rude refused to tell me whether his guy was a PI or some kind of neighborhood man on the street. I didn't take it as a good sign when we pulled into the potholed parking lot of a Mexican restaurant. From the design of the building, the place had once been a pizza chain franchise. Only now it had been painted blue and white, which made it look like a giant iced bakery cupcake.

"Here's our first stop," Rude said, killing the engine.

"First?"

"There's always at least one more. You get information here, dude —but not the answers."

"Since when did you start talking in riddles?"

"Since we came here. You have to be careful what you say about this guy and his people."

His people? "This should be fun."

"Just let me do the talking. You got something to say, check with me before you say it."

Rude wouldn't get out of the car until I agreed, so I did.

Inside, the restaurant smelled right, and it had the standard hostess podium with menus and rolled silverware—but it played as weird as it did from the outside. We were the only people there, for starters. I couldn't see anyone, not even waiters. No tables; only all booths, each one outfitted with plastic daisies in a vase.

The walls were covered in crosses. All shapes, all sizes. So many in fact, I couldn't help wondering what the owners were afraid of.

The ceiling took the cake. Half of it had been painted in black and orange, full of fire and brimstone and pitchforks. The other half, blue sky and clouds with angels and harps. Heaven and hell.

What kind of guy could we be meeting in a place like this?

Rude shot me a helping of side-eye. "Don't embarrass me, dude."

"Wouldn't dream of it."

After another uncomfortable moment, a door swung open at the far end of the place. A skinny Latina girl in a white shirt/black pants hostess uniform met us at the podium.

"Two?" she asked.

Rude nodded. "For Oscar's section."

Oscar's section was not in the dining room. The girl took us into the inferno of the kitchen, past Latinx and Korean line cooks in chef's clothes and ball caps, sweat dripping down their faces, into a back room with faded posters papering the walls and a concrete floor—I recognized Selena's face and Frida Kahlo's, but none of the others. The only furniture was a single table with four chairs.

The girl left us alone with a couple of menus. And came back ten seconds later with water, chips, and salsa before she disappeared again.

Rude studied the menu. "What are you having?"

"We're staying for dinner?" I couldn't stay for dinner, especially if we had another stop after this. I knew I'd be cutting the time close coming here, but I hadn't counted on slicing and dicing it, too.

"You don't eat, you insult the guy."

Rude had to be kidding. Also, he could quit calling Oscar "the guy." "How late are we going to be here?"

"Until we're done."

Very helpful. I was going to be in even more serious trouble with my dad.

Halfway through our cheese enchiladas, Oscar finally showed up. Joe Normal, not scary at all. And a lot younger than I expected. Not that I was great at guessing, but I'd lay bets on late twenties.

Oscar's skin was dark brown, his thick black hair cut close. He wore a crisp red corduroy button-down, jeans with the crease ironed in, and sprung cowboy boots. When he sat down across from us, I couldn't help but notice his broad shoulders, the solid muscle of his arms, the calluses on his hands. He worked for a living.

He didn't smile. In fact, he looked mad. Also, he ignored me completely.

"You know you're only to come in here once a week," Oscar said to Rude. "What's it been? Three days?"

Rude took a deep breath. "It's an emergency. And it's not for me."

"Also against our agreement," Oscar said.

"He's got a couple of guys after him. They're pretending to be cops."

Oscar tapped a finger on the table. "I can see that without your telling me."

He could? How?

"You'll pay the penalty for breaking the agreement. And the fee for your friend here," Oscar said. It wasn't a question.

"What penalty?" I asked.

"Shut. Up. Kev."

All this mysterious crap. Agreements. Rules. Shut up, Kev.

I didn't like it. I pushed back from the table, chair legs scraping on the concrete. "Time to go."

Oscar met and held my gaze. "Hearing things lately?"

Fuck me.

It had been an honest question, and meant to keep me in my seat. It worked.

"You are, aren't you?" Oscar asked.

"Not today."

Oscar leaned forward. "When did it start?"

I crooked my thumb at Rude. "His house."

"At the party."

Again with the question that wasn't. "How do you know all this stuff?"

"I saw it."

"As in, you were there?"

"As in, that's what he does," Rude said.

I took a good, hard look at Oscar's eyes. Didn't catch anything special about them.

"I'm a seer," Oscar said. "But it doesn't always have a lot to do with my eyeballs. It's just a term."

"And that means what to someone like me?"

"You're straightforward," Oscar said. "I like that about you. Others might not so much. Check yourself before you get impatient with them."

How else was I supposed to be? I folded my arms across my chest. "What's a seer?"

"A person who's in contact with the other realms—places where humans dare not go, where other kinds of beings live."

I stared at him, in case he'd actually just said a bunch of stuff about humans and other beings, whatever they were.

"I'm talking about the Fae," Oscar said. "Faeries."

For real? "Tinkerbell?"

"Far from it. They're bigger, for one thing. A lot bigger. For another, they're not cute. They're seductive and treacherous and they don't operate by the same rules humans do."

He had to be joking. What was I supposed to do—play along? I opened my mouth to snark, then snapped it shut before the first word rolled off my tongue. Man didn't look like he was kidding. He looked serious as hell. He'd known things about me and where I'd been without Rude or me telling him.

Rude trusted him. I could try to do that, too.

"They give you information?" I asked.

"They do," Oscar said.

All the spit in my mouth dried up. "What do they tell you about the things I hear?"

"It happens when there's danger," Oscar said. "And sometimes there's a residual effect, where you keep on hearing thoughts for a while afterwards."

I thought about Scott (the betraying asshole). I'd saved his life and maybe the life of someone else he might've met on the road. If I hadn't heard Scott's thoughts—or if I hadn't listened to them—something awful could've happened.

I'd heard Rude's neighbor. If I hadn't, nearly everyone at the party would've been busted.

If I hadn't heard the cops—

This thing that was happening to me, whatever it was, had done nothing so far but help me. And it wasn't all the time. I'd heard nothing from my dad. And not a single thought all day today while my rep at school, such as it was, tanked.

I took a deep breath. "Define 'danger.'"

Oscar knocked on the table once for each word: "Imminent. Mortal. Danger."

My stomach did a somersault. My enchilada rested in there like a brick. "And what do you want me to do with this information?"

"Use it," Oscar said. "Or don't. Your choice."

"I didn't have a choice on Saturday."

"But you did," Rude said. "I just can't imagine you doing anything but what you did. You're stand-up, man."

Hearing that only made me feel more nauseated. Also vaguely pink around the ears.

Oscar pushed his chair away from the table. Leaving so soon, when I still had hundreds of unanswered questions I couldn't even think of, much less ask.

"Your choice," Oscar said again. "If you use the information you glean, be prepared. The people you help may not appreciate it."

No shit.

"You may end up in trouble," Oscar continued. "You'd better get good at making up stories, because nine times out of ten you won't be able to tell your father or your principal or the cops how you know what you know."

I could lie. I had some skills in the area of obfuscation, too. "About those cops."

Oscar pulled a folded sheet of notebook paper from his back pocket. "Go to this address tonight. Make sure you're there before midnight, or all bets are off."

I took the paper from him. "What's the hurry?"

"She won't be there for long after midnight," Oscar said, and headed for the door.

Huh?

Oscar paused in the doorway. "One more thing—if you don't use the information you receive, eventually you will stop hearing it."

Seeing as I felt like I could throw up any time now, maybe that would be the way to go.

"God forbid," Oscar said, "that it abandons you when you need it the most."

"Thank you," Rude said.

Oscar nodded. "You will come back tomorrow night and pay that penalty. Don't forget, Rudolph, or all bets are off."

Oscar left us alone.

It took me a couple of minutes to feel my feet on the floor. And Rude didn't move an inch, either.

I cleared my throat. "What does 'all bets are off' mean?"

"Imminent. Mortal. Danger."

"Jesus, man. What kind of place is this?"

"The kind where they grant wishes."

Wishes were good things, weren't they?

Rude held out his hand. "Give me the paper."

Unfolding it, we read the street and number written in red ink that reminded me of blood. I didn't recognize the place.

"It's in the warehouse district downtown," Rude said. And he didn't look happy about it. In fact, he looked scared.

I'd never seen him like that. Rude was fearless. At least, he was supposed to be.

"What's there, at this warehouse or whatever?" I asked.

"A girl. If we're lucky."

What was so frightening about a girl? And what if we weren't lucky?

Rude checked his watch. "What time does your dad go to bed?"

The last couple of nights, who knew? "Probably by nine," I said. "Or at least he'll be in his room by then."

"Then I'll pick you up at nine. That's cutting it close, but it's better than if you can't get out at all."

I planned it all out in my head. The right timing. Go out the window or the front door? What would I say if I got caught coming or going?

Rude tapped his watch. "It's six now."

"I'm late."

Dad would be home by now, wondering where the hell I was, why there was no dinner on the table, why I'd disobeyed his law. And probably whether he'd be having another visit from the cops.

I had to get past Dad. And I had to get out of the house on time to go see a terrifying girl in some alley downtown on the orders of a restaurant owner who claimed to see faeries.

My life had taken a serious turn. Question was, where would it go from here?

CHAPTER 8

DAD BEAT me home, like I'd figured. But instead of finding him ready to beat my ass, I walked in to peace and quiet so loud, it freaked me out.

Dust motes floated in the air. Puddles of light from the living room lamps looked deep enough to drown in. Someone drove by outside, the engine roaring, then fading to gone. The chill of conditioned air raised goose bumps on my arms.

I checked the kitchen. A cutting board on the counter held whole wheat bread crusts, a dollop of mayo, and strips of iceberg lettuce—Dad had made himself a sandwich. The sole remaining six-pack of beer had been plucked from the fridge. The clock on the wall ticked like a time bomb.

The door to Dad's room was closed. No sound at all issued from inside. No TV. No music. But I felt the weight of his presence. The anger in his silence practically seethed through the cracks between the door and the frame.

He'd never been this pissed at me before.

What if it wasn't about me? What if something was wrong with him? Maybe he was hurt. In trouble.

Amend that—Dad had been in trouble since Mom died. Maybe

things had gotten worse. Maybe it had something to do with what was happening to me. I didn't know how, or why I thought it. I only knew I felt worried in a way I hadn't felt in a long time.

I balled up my fist, ready to knock, but couldn't bring myself to do it.

I'd been afraid for Dad before, not that I'd told anyone. Because, my dad? Should be the grown-up, on top of stuff, in charge. The one who if you screwed up too bad would fix the problem. Dads did that. Mine tried, when he could. And that was something. Not enough, but something.

The drinking hadn't just gotten out of control. Dad didn't get drunk to forget or to stop feeling things so much—in the beginning, it'd been like that. But as days and weeks and months passed, something had shifted in him. My father hadn't taken handful of pills or stepped off a high place or sliced his wrists, but he'd basically tried to kill himself with alcohol. Was still trying.

Dad had no friends. No family other than me. No one was coming to the rescue except Social Services, and I couldn't call them. I couldn't do that to him.

I'd never told a soul, because who would understand? Nobody, that was who.

I sighed.

Better to leave him alone right now. If he was too pissed to talk to me now, I'd wait until the anger passed. Better to thank all the powers that be for my luck, not having to deal with it tonight. Do my thing and be ready to jam when Rude pulled up.

But I stood and listened outside the bedroom door for what felt like forever. Finally, I heard the hiss of the shower in the master bath. That gave me permission to walk away.

I finished my Grendel essay. Couldn't concentrate on the Stat homework, all of the problems on page thirty-eight. I felt hungry again and microwaved a frozen pizza, but didn't even taste the cardboard crust and waxy cheese on the way down. My nerves ratcheted tighter every half hour on the hour until Rude texted to say he'd be by in five.

No reason to sneak out, not with Dad settled into his room for the night. I set the timer on my desk lamp, the one we'd always used when Mom had been alive and we went out of town. If it could fool a burglar into thinking the house was occupied, then it ought to fool my dad.

For a heartbeat, I considered just walking out, but if something was really wrong with Dad, and he came in and found me missing—I couldn't finish the thought. I scribbled a explanation on a torn sheet of notebook paper and left it front-and-center on my desk. I might be in the worst trouble of my life when I got home, but at least there'd be no calling of friends and hospitals in the meantime.

If Dad heard my footsteps in the hallway or the ring when I pulled my house keys off the brass holder by the front door or the squeal of the hinges, he gave no sign.

Rude's Explorer hulked in the driveway, casting a big shadow in the glow of the streetlamp. The big guy had killed the headlights, but the engine made plenty of noise. Enough to draw a dad out of the house to ask his grounded kid where the hell he thought he was going, if that dad were paying attention. If that dad cared.

Nothing happened.

I swallowed hard and climbed in, into a heavy-metal wall of sound, and slammed the door as loud as I could.

Still no sign from the house.

"Something wrong?" Rude asked.

Everything. But I shook my head. Dad would be there to deal with when I got home. Until then, I had other problems to handle.

The drive into downtown took up half an hour. The freeway dumped us into the deserted business district, into claustrophobia-inducing steel and glass and concrete canyons. Far down the way, the blue-neon-lit Ferris wheel beckoned, promising aquariums and restaurants and clubs. That was where all the people would be. There, and across the way at the fancy theaters where the ballet and the symphony played.

We turned away from all that, toward the deserted baseball stadium and the warehouses, driving one-way roads narrowed with orange construction barrels. We passed a landscaped park with a sign that said something about UNDER CONSTRUCTION / OPENING NEXT SPRING, and parking lots with knee-high weeds and potholed pavement.

I didn't like it. Then again, what had I expected? That Oscar would send us to a sunshiny place?

Rude turned onto a dead-end street tight enough to be an alley, red brick warehouses with boarded-up windows growing up three stories on either side. All dark, no sign of life that I could see except for the rusted yellow school bus that rested at the back of the alley. Faint light shone inside the thing's windows and open door.

"Oscar sent us to a school bus?" I asked.

Rude killed the radio and the ignition. He lit up a smoke with trembling fingers. "It's a very special bus, dude."

I stepped out of the car, Rude scrambling to catch me. In the shadow of the warehouses, I saw hardly any stars, fewer even than at home. The red light of a passing plane winked overhead. A breeze kicked up, sweeping a crumpled newspaper across the asphalt. My sneakers crunched on broken beer bottles. The temperature dropped the closer I drew to the bus. The cold knifed through my clothes.

Just like a horror movie. Any second now, we'd get our guts handed to us.

Rude jogged past me, stopping before he got to the door and motioning for me to do the same.

"Oscar sent us," he called.

No one answered.

I stepped closer to him. "You sure she's home?"

"Just wait, dude."

A wind blew again—this time from inside the bus. The hairs on my arms stood up.

"That's our cue." Rude climbed the steps.

I half-expected him to get struck by lightning or vanish into thin air or get stabbed.

None of that happened.

Rude glanced over his shoulder. "It's all right."

He climbed the steps into the bus, and I didn't wait to be told twice to follow. No way was I staying out here by myself.

Walking into the bus felt like stepping into a time warp. The girl who lived there had to be a hippy. Or else hippies had exploded all over the inside of the bus.

The sweet scents of pot and patchouli incense permeated the whole place. Tiny, tinkling wind chimes hung near the windows. Every available ceiling space had been papered with black-light posters, so many I couldn't make out the images on them. Along the edges of the center aisle, candles burned in deep glass jars, their glowing wicks almost drowned in melted wax.

Bicycle handlebars and chains and pedals lay strewn on the ripped vinyl bench seats. Except on every third seat, where pillows and blankets had been gathered into piles to protect unframed oil paintings on stretched canvases. Good paintings.

The longer we stood there, the thicker the air got. And charged. With electricity. The kind that shocked. Or if it got strong enough, the kind that could do some damage. It wasn't enough that the hair on my arms stood up. All the hair on my head did, too. Rude got lucky, having that buzz cut.

Rude cocked his head, listening. To what?

"She wants a song," he said. "She wants it like an offering, or we have to leave."

Without another word, he launched into an off-key version of Linkin Park's "No More Sorrow."

I'd never heard him sing before, and never wanted to again. The whole thing couldn't end fast enough.

When it did, the quality of the air had changed. I could breathe better. I didn't feel like I might be electrocuted any minute.

And there was a girl at the back of the bus. A girl with actual attached gossamer wings.

CHAPTER 9

S HAGGY RED HAIR STREAKED with purple framed the porcelain skin of her face. Her violet-blue eyes glinted with—I could only call it *power*, no matter how fantasy-movie that sounded.

She wore a sleeveless, gauzy black dress that had been shredded on the bottom. As she walked toward us, I could see a lot of leg and a pair of scuffed black combat boots. Her dress dragged through the burning candles, but didn't catch fire. And those wings? They looked as if they belonged to someone more delicate, more angelic. I could see the muscles in her shoulders move, and blood coursing rhythmically in the veins of the wings.

I stared. I couldn't think of anything else to do.

She didn't return my gaze, though. She only had eyes for Rude.

"What do you want?" she asked, in a voice that raked through me like fingernails on a chalkboard. Definitely not delicate.

Rude took a deep breath. "Your help."

"How obvious," she said. "Do you want a spell cast? Information? A curse? Do tell."

A curse? I tried to step back, to put a little more distance between myself and the magic curser, but my feet wouldn't move right.

Rude crooked a thumb in my direction. "It's for him."

"But you made the offering, Rudolph Diamond Davies III."

"I want you to help him," Rude repeated.

"You know it doesn't work that way," she said.

It took me a second to get my mouth to work right. "What way does it work?"

The girl turned toward me, and I wished I'd zipped my lip. The full force of her gaze burned me, and not in a good way. "Do you want to bargain for yourself, Kevin Xavier Landon?"

In two seconds, she ruined all the work I'd done since kindergarten to make my friends believe I didn't have a middle name. Also, it didn't help that I blushed.

"Xavier?" Rude whispered.

"Shut up."

The girl waited for an answer.

Be careful, Rude thought.

I heard that loud and clear. Oscar's words scrolled across my mind, that the ability to hear thoughts went hand in hand with imminent mortal danger.

And on the heels of those verbal gems, the realization that Oscar hadn't told me the thing that mattered most. He hadn't said anything about how to interpret what I heard.

Rude wanted me to watch myself. That meant whatever I decided to do—or not—could get one or both of us killed. Not awesome.

"What does 'bargain' mean?" I asked.

"If you break it, you die," the girl said.

Helpful. Down to brass tacks, direct was the best way to have a conversation. "I tell you what I want, and then you tell me what I need to do to get it, right?"

She shook her head. "We deal first. Then we work together as friends."

Rude pleaded, *Please be careful, man.*

I wished I could shut that thought and the sound of it out of my brain. Rude, begging. It threatened to leech away what little confidence I could summon.

It hit me that Rude could've said something out loud. He could've warned me off like that, or changed the subject, or called the whole thing off. It looked like he was trying to, only his lips just quivered instead of forming words.

I forced myself to keep talking. Hopefully, I would ask the right questions and I'd get the answers I needed. "Why?"

"To decide whether I'll be working with you at all, I have to know you."

"And I'll know something about you," I said. "An even trade."

Dude! Rude thought so hard, it seared the inside of my brain.

I closed my eyes a half-second, steadied myself.

"As you wish," the girl said, in a tone that told me I'd screwed up big-time. She had one over on me, and I was too stupid to understand what I'd given up.

She can't lie, Rude thought. *And she can tell if you're lying.*

I gave a silent prayer of thanks for that piece of info. "You first."

She nodded. "One night of your life. It need not be this night."

In human time, Rude thought.

"In human time," I said.

The girl flashed me a very disconcerting, very human smile. "All right. With that condition, do you agree?"

"Not yet," I said. "What do you want it for?"

"It won't hurt you."

That just pissed me off. "Not afraid of you."

And I wasn't. Not in that moment.

She cocked her head.

"I get to say what I want in return first," I said. "That's how trading's done."

"Not here," she said. "I'll give you what I deem fit. It's always equitable."

If Rude was right and she couldn't lie, then I'd have to take that at face value. "What do you deem fit?"

She moved toward me, chilling the space to freezing as she went. My breath frosted the air. But hers didn't. She didn't appear to breathe at all.

She leaned into me and opened a mouth full of too-sharp teeth and I swore to God she was going to take a bite out of me.

She spoke into my ear instead. For me alone to hear.

"My name is Simone," she said. "You may not speak that name aloud in front of any other living being."

I whispered. "Not even Rude?"

Rude stood only a foot away. He might even have heard what she said. His hearing could be good enough. It could happen.

She shook her head.

"Not even in an emergency?"

"Not even then," she said. "It's strictly between you and me. And when you call me, I'll show. That's guaranteed."

And that was worth what? "That's all?"

"That's the deal, Kevin Xavier Landon." She raised her left arm and leaned against the metal partition behind the driver's seat. She had a tattoo there, a red and blue sparrow. And a banner in black and gray that said Rock 'n' Roll Forever.

What kind of supernatural creature had tattoos like that? Maybe a singer in a rock band.

I opened my mouth to get a bigger bang for my buck. To ask her for her full name, and the other questions I'd come here with, but never got the chance.

The girl and her ink and the bus grayed out. I tipped over. I couldn't even move a finger, much less reach out and break the fall.

I expected to hit the floor, but just kept on falling into the dark.

When I came to—when both of us swam out of unconsciousness— we lay in the street beside the car. The bus was gone.

I could've tricked myself into believing I'd hallucinated it all, from Rude's nu-metal vocals to the name the fae girl had given me. But the asphalt in front of us was stained with freshly leaked oil and the name hovered on the edge of my tongue.

It took a minute to stand up and brush myself off. I felt like I should say something, but didn't know what.

Rude made four attempts at running his mouth, fifth time the charm. "You okay, dude?"

Not even close, but I nodded anyway. "Where'd the bus go?"

"To Faery. That's where it always goes when it disappears, according to Oscar. Always before dawn."

I stared at him.

"It's no weirder than anything else that happened tonight," he said.

I gave him the point and shrugged.

"So what did she tell you?"

"Her name," I said. "Doesn't seem like much compared to a whole night of my life."

"Some people figure it's worth its weight in gold," Rude said. "Or more, definitely more."

"Who's some people?"

Rude studied his shoes. "Guys who work with the fae their whole lives and still never hear a name."

That sounded personal. "Like you?"

"Maybe."

Meaning *yes*.

I didn't feel superior. I felt like a dick for having something my friend didn't. Especially since Rude had stuck his neck out so far to help me. "Why do you think I got so lucky?"

"She likes you, man."

What kind of answer was that? "She probably likes lots of people."

"No, man," Rude said. "She *likes* you."

I didn't even know how to take that. "No."

"Dude, she doesn't smile at everybody."

"That smile—does it always look so sharp?"

Rude shook his head.

"We take our good news where we can get it," I said.

He laughed even though what I'd said wasn't that funny.

The sound was contagious, and it drew me in. I'd never needed to laugh so badly—if for no other reason than to camouflage the heavy case of the shakes I felt coming on. It exhausted me so much, I didn't think I had any energy left to freak out.

"I need to ask you something," I said when I could finally talk again.

"Shoot, dude."

"How'd you get involved in all this?"

"That's a long story. Maybe I'll tell you the whole tale sometime."

"Really?"

"Really."

"You're not crazy?" I asked.

"Not that I know of."

I smelled water in the air. Fast-moving clouds obscured the sky. Lightning lit them from behind, like a photonegative. Far-off thunder rumbled. We put ourselves in the car for the drive home.

Rude turned the key in the ignition. The dash clock glowed to life. 3:17.

I whistled. "We couldn't have been in that bus more than half an hour. We must've been passed out in the street a helluva long time."

"It was the bus," Rude said. "Bus keeps Faery time."

"So if we'd stayed in there, say, all night?"

"Earliest we'd have come out? Probably dinner time tomorrow. Not that it's an exact calculation. It's kind of muzzy."

Muzzy. Good word for how my head felt. I buckled up nice and slow. The first drops of rain sprinkled the windshield. "So that thing about human time you were thinking at me?"

"Didn't want you to end up like some of those guys in the fairy tales—fall asleep in Faery and wake up in a hundred years."

I shivered. "What happens now?"

"Fuck if I know, Kevin."

Rude gave me a minute to let it all sink in. Then he turned up the tunes and peeled out, leaving a trail of rubber on the road.

CHAPTER 10

I WOKE IN THE MORNING without any memory of the rest of the drive home, or of falling into bed with my clothes still on. I stank of Mexican food and Rude's cigarettes and rotting school bus and patchouli and whatever had been on the street by the car where Rude and I had passed out.

Another smell crept beneath all those things: something warm and dark. Simone and her gossamer wings. The power that had crackled around her. Magic.

How could you smell magic?

I didn't have a lot of time to get ready for school, where I so did not want to be today. Yesterday's awfulness aside, two hours' sleep would have me face-down on a desk by second period. Now, it just made for an unbalanced walk to the shower and a slightly less groggy march to the kitchen, where Dad sat at the breakfast table, normal as you please, reading the paper. By the looks of it, having chowed down on fruit, yogurt, and toast.

"Morning," I said, normally.

I waited for him to return the greeting. With the way things had been going, I should've known better. Long wait, standing in line for those skates at the ice rink in hell.

"I looked for you in your room last night, after ten," he said. "I wanted to check on you, tell you good night. Where were you, Kevin?"

"I left a note."

"I didn't believe what you wrote."

"Am I a habitual liar?"

"You're acting funny, Kevin."

"And you'd notice that how?"

He ignored that. He took a breath and started again. "Where were you?"

"Rude's. Like the note said." I needed coffee. Lots of coffee. I pulled the largest mug from the cabinet and tried to pour without spilling all over the pristine, white-tiled counter.

"I called his house, Kevin. His parents don't remember seeing you. Or him, for that matter."

I bobbled the coffee pot and the mug, splattering liquid all over the counter. I grabbed the sponge from over by the sink and tried to clear the cobwebs from my synapses while I mopped up the spill.

There was nothing I could say to fix this. I could only tell the truth —no, as close to the truth as I could come.

"We went out."

Dad folded the paper and set it on the table. "And the part where you're grounded and not supposed to do that? Did you think about that?"

"Yeah, I did."

"And you chose to disregard it."

I shook my head. "It wasn't like that."

"You want to tell me what it was like?"

I guzzled coffee and burned the crap out of my tongue. "School sucked. Everyone thinks I had something to do with that girl dying at Rude's house. Even Scott blew me off."

"I'm sorry about Scott."

Not a word about the other stuff. Did he think I deserved all that?

"I just needed to blow off some steam."

"You're still grounded. Doesn't change that fact."

I nodded.

"I'll be picking you up from school today." Dad pushed away from the table. "And tomorrow, and the day after that."

Things were bad enough. Now this? Of all the mortifying things I'd never live down. "You don't need to do that."

"Obviously, I do."

"C'mon, Dad. Don't do this to me."

"You did it to yourself, Kevin."

Because I hadn't followed the letter of the law. Well, it was a stupid law. "Can't you cut me some slack?"

"You want slack? Next time, don't get caught."

In what universe did a father say something like that? Mom would never have even considered it. It would've been about The Principle of the Thing, her words. Not about doing what you could get away with.

Everything would be different if she was here. If she hadn't died.

I took a deep breath and blew it out slow, measured. Controlled. I wanted my father back the way he'd been. Before.

Might as well wish for the Easter Bunny to be real. Or the monster under the bed. Or faeries. A hysterical laugh clawed up the back of my throat. I held it in and rubbed my temples. Any minute now my head would explode.

I shut down that whole train of thought. Period. End of thinking. Never to come up again, please and thanks.

"Is that it?" I asked, finally. "You gonna drive me to school, too?"

"I have to go to work. I trust you can get yourself there." With that, he stood up and walked out of the house.

I topped off my half-empty mug, even though there couldn't be enough coffee in the entire world to wake me up from this nightmare.

I threw on a sweatshirt over my tee and slipped into sneakers, shoved my English assignment into my backpack.

Grendel the outcast.

Hard not to see parallels and metaphors and all that kind of crap. I wasn't an outcast. If I told myself that enough times, maybe it would turn out to be true.

On my way out the door, phone in hand, I noticed I'd turned off my cell—probably sometime last night, though I didn't remember it and would never have committed that kind of blasphemy.

A lot of texts and three actual phone messages. All of them from Amy.

Hi, this is Amy, calling for Kevin. Kevin, call me. Followed by a garbled number.

Hey, Kevin. Amy. Britt told me something today I wanted to check out with you. Can you call me? Anytime before midnight is okay. Thanks.

The words "Britt told me something" had my hackles up. The way Britt and Zoe walked behind Amy and me on the way to class. The sideways looks they gave us—me. I tried not to worry about what the "something" might be.

The next message? My heart sank. All the goodwill had bled out of Amy's voice.

Hi, Kevin. I need to talk to you about our plans for Friday. See you tomorrow, okay?

The walk to school seemed to take forever. The houses on either side watched me, their empty windows like dark eyes. Hedges of red-tipped photinia and azaleas walled off yards like prison bars. I passed the four-way stop where the block split without seeing a soul.

With a quarter block left to go, I checked out the busy four lanes of traffic on Rice Boulevard I'd have to cross, and the front of the school.

Buses filled the driveway, none of them rusted and full of chimes and strange, tattooed fae girls. People sat on the lawn, doing last-minute homework and eating snack-machine breakfasts and passing rumors.

Sometimes Amy hung out there on the grass. I didn't see her this morning, though. Not that I didn't want to. I just didn't want her to treat me like something she scraped off the bottom of her shoe—or worse, like as if she felt sorry for me. Then again, if she'd wanted to do that, she could have just blown me off with a text.

Rude appeared at the corner, one second not there and the next solid and real, on the neighborhood side of Rice. Resplendent in today's green Hawaiian shirt, no backpack. In fact, nothing at all that would indicate he planned on going into that building across the way. He smoked a cigarette while I closed the distance between us.

"Got a proposition for you, man," he said with a glint in his eye.

I needed more trouble like I needed to be grounded some more, with new and improved restrictions.

Rude didn't beat around the bush. "We'd have to ditch."

When I didn't show up for class, someone in the administration office might call my dad. If by some miracle they didn't do that, then I'd still have to write an excuse and forge his signature. Too many pitfalls.

Worse than what my dad might do if I got caught? Losing my chance at a scholarship.

I sighed. "You know I can't do that, man."

"I know. A-student and all that. But there's something I've got to show you."

"What do you mean, 'got to'?"

"Got a call from Oscar," Rude said.

"At eight o'clock in the morning?"

"Five, actually. Fucker woke me up." Disturbed him, too, by the looks of it.

People only called at times like that when they had to. When they needed bailing out. Or when someone had died. "So, what's the emergency?"

"It's about your dad," Rude said.

As if. "You mean the guy who knew I sneaked out last night? That guy?"

"That sucks, Kev."

"No shit. Didn't you get in trouble?"

"Nope."

"But my dad said he called your house. He busted you with your folks."

"They were up when I got home, waiting for me. Five minutes later, they went to bed and forgot all about my being gone—and about my being with you—just like that." Rude snapped his fingers.

I heard the awe in my own voice. "How?"

"It's a charm Oscar gave me. Keeps the parents off my back when I can. When it's important."

"What's that mean?"

"It means I can only use it when there's not a lot of people involved. That's why I couldn't use it when the cops raided the party. Too many of us, too many of them. I can't work on that many memories at once. Also, I don't use it unless I have to. It has a big price. All magic has a price."

"Like what you're set to pay Oscar tonight? You gonna tell me what it is?"

"Chop wood, carry water," Rude said. "Chores and crap. At least it has an upside. The good luck rubs off on me, or at least it seems to stick around a while."

A light bulb went off. I grinned. "That have anything to do with why you can get away with smoking at school?"

"Maybe so." Rude changed the subject. "But seriously, dude. About your dad."

I shifted the weight of my backpack. "Oscar doesn't know my dad."

"He doesn't have to," Rude said. "Remember that stuff he talked about? He's a seer. He just knows things."

Because the fae told him. Fae like Simone.

"What exactly did he tell you about my father?" I asked.

"He gave me a time and a place and said be there. Around ten. We should see something important."

And for something that vague I was supposed to skip class and risk screwing up my life even more? "Is it bad?"

"I don't know, man."

Yeah, but with Oscar and the fae, how could it be good?

"My ride's one block over," Rude said. "We'll be back before anyone misses us."

That was outright bullshit. "If they call our parents?"

"They won't," Rude said.

"Your famous luck?"

"Maybe."

Again with the bullshit.

I had to choose. Go or don't. Find out whatever Oscar had flagged about my dad or not. Worry about myself or worry about my father.

Shit.

I gave the front lawn of the school one last look and saw Amy with her girlfriends. She had on a dark green cardigan with a lacy something underneath, a long black skirt with rivets at the hem, her boots. And she'd braided her hair today. She looked amazing.

"We've gotta move now," Rude said.

I didn't have time to go over and talk to her. I pulled the phone out of my pocket and texted her.

Got yr messages. Tied up last nite. Xplain later.

I watched her receive and read. She looked up and met my gaze. After a moment, she texted back. *QT.*

Anyone asked her, she'd deny having seen us. That would have to be good enough for now.

Rude turned on his heel. I followed, kissing normal—and maybe my not-yet relationship—goodbye.

CHAPTER 11

W E DROVE WEST. Until we made it out of the immediate
vicinity of school, beyond the crossing guards and the cops
aiming their radar guns at unsuspecting school zone speeders, I felt
sure someone with authority would flag us down. I couldn't stop
fidgeting, so I tried to do it as inconspicuously as possible.

There was a lot of new and scary stuff going on. I could feel overwhelm speeding toward me like a freight train from the blinding
headlight to the ground trembling beneath my feet. I didn't know how
much more I could deal with.

Once we cleared the neighborhood, I expected Rude to turn
around. After all, my dad worked downtown, which was in the oppo-
site direction. But no. Rude hadn't exactly said we'd be going there. I'd
just assumed.

"So where the hell are we going?" I asked.

"To a parking lot across the street from the restaurant Oscar
works out of."

"What does it have to do with my dad?"

"He'll be there," Rude said.

"He'll be at work. Between eight-thirty and five-thirty, that's
where he is every day."

Rude lifted both hands from the wheel long enough to shrug. "Hey, don't take my word for it. See it with your own eyeballs. Oscar said you'd need to. That's why we're going."

Oscar said. "What is it with you and Oscar? How come when he says jump you ask how high?"

"He's my teacher. I'm learning from him how to be a seer."

I hadn't expected that. I didn't know what I'd expected, exactly. "How do you learn something like that?"

"You ever see that movie *The Karate Kid*?"

"Some of it."

"You know all that 'wax-on, wax-off' stuff?"

"Vaguely."

"Well, it's mostly like that. Like I said before: chop wood, carry water. I keep feeling like he hasn't taught me squat yet, like he's testing me to see whether I've got what it takes."

"How long has this been going on?"

"Almost a year," Rude said.

I'd never guessed—but how would I even have begun? I was still trying to wrap my head around magic and faeries in the real world, which meant reimagining what the word "real" actually meant. The kind of secret Rude had kept was monumental.

How did you reconcile the Rudolph Diamond Davies III, who threw parties when his parents went out of town and who smoked at school without being hassled by security, with a guy studying to be a mystical whoosit? Life-of-the-party Rude Davies, the faery seer?

When had Rude gotten so serious? How much else had I missed about him? About everything?

"How did you meet Oscar?" I asked.

"I was at the Ritual Room downtown, you know?"

I nodded. The dance club, the one open to eighteen and under on Thursdays. Where else could you get your flashlight on with Parliament Funkadelic one minute and industrialize with Nine Inch Nails the next? Old-school heaven. Plus, live bands playing new music every night after twelve. Everyone knew that place.

"Oscar was there, waiting for a band to hit the stage. The Wild

Hunt—that was the name of the band. Anyway, he saw me and kept on looking at me, you know, like people just don't do. I figured he was coming on to me or something. He gave me a business card. Then I *knew* he was coming on to me."

"Sounds promising."

"Dude," he said. "He's too old for me."

I raised a brow.

"Don't even think about setting me up with anyone," he said.

"I wasn't." I hadn't gotten that far.

"It's not that I'm not interested. It's just that I'm not interested."

"I have no idea what that means, man."

"It means I notice girls and dudes, but I don't want to go out with anybody right now."

I filed the info in the back of my brain for when Rude changed his mind about dating.

"Anyway," Rude said, "I tossed the card on my way out the door. A week later, I stopped at the restaurant to eat, no particular reason other than I could've wolfed down a whale. He sat down across the booth from me. I thought he was crazy."

"I know the feeling," I said. "Do you think he could be bullshitting you?"

"That's just it," Rude said. "I won't know until the year's up—a year and a day, actually. Then I'll either learn something serious, or he'll say, Rudolph, it's been real, don't come back."

"He calls you Rudolph?"

"Yeah," Rude said. "He's just about the only one who does. Except for my mom."

Mrs. Davies wouldn't know a nickname if it bit her in the ass, true. "So, why do you want to be a faery seer?"

Rude flushed. As in red cheeks, back of the neck, the whole enchilada. "Who doesn't want superpowers?"

I started to raise my hand—but Rude cut me off by pointing out the Parking Lot of Doom as we passed it.

He didn't pull right in; he looped the block and came at it through the neighborhood rather than from the main drag. That way, we could park in the back of the newly poured asphalt lot, in the shade of the pampas grass along the chain-link fence, without being seen by anyone who happened to be idling at the front.

I gaped at the Suburban, its back windshield cleaner than usual after last night's rain, windows down. Clearly visible inside? The top of my dad's head, with that one strand sticking up because of the cowlick, blowing in the cross breeze. Dad was eating something that resembled a croissant sandwich, slurping coffee from a large Styrofoam cup.

Goddamn him, I heard clear as a goddamn bell.

Dad's thoughts. Jesus H. Christ in a sidecar. "What's he doing here?"

"He's watching Oscar," Rude said.

"You've gotta be kidding."

Rude crossed his heart. "He was out here yesterday, too."

"But what about his job?"

"Maybe he's calling in sick, Kev. He's got time coming to him, right?"

Not that I kept that close a track on my dad's work life, but that was possible. Dad took a sick day every few weeks. He just got overwhelmed. Stayed home all day, away from people. Or so I'd always believed.

A thought skittered across my mind that I couldn't un-think: maybe Dad had been fired or quit. If that were true, then I had a lot more to worry about than Amy and school and the cops-who-weren't and the rock 'n' roll fae girl and her bus and what on earth Dad could be doing in this parking lot when he should be accounting for some lawyer's travel expenses. Like, you know, whether we were going to eat next week and how we were going to pay the bills.

I. Could. Not. Go. There.

Stick to the problem at hand, please and thank you.

I cleared my throat. "Why is he watching Oscar?"

"We think he's looking for an opportunity to get to him."

"What does that mean?"

"Means your dad wants to hurt Oscar."

I shook my head. "That doesn't make sense."

"You know what I told you about the cops?" Rude asked.

I blinked. "What do they have to do with this?"

Rude spoke slowly. Like he was schoolin' a dummy. Which pissed me off so much, it made me not want to listen.

"What'd I say to you about them?" Rude asked.

"That they're not cops." I made the mental leap. "Are you saying that's not really my father?"

"Something's off with him," Rude said. "Oscar said he's—"

"What?"

"Broken." Rude turned toward me. "I know that sounds bad."

"He hasn't been himself lately."

"What does 'lately' mean?"

"The last year," I said.

"Your mom?"

I dug my fingernails into the armrest. I wanted out of the car. "He's just upset about what happened with the fake law. He's just pissed off about opening the door to let them in and having to think something happened to me, just like with my mom. That's all it is."

"You should talk to Oscar."

"I'm not going within five feet of that dude. He's certifiable. And so are you. I'll prove it."

"How, Kevin?"

By marching over to talk to my dad, who had no reason on earth to be sitting in this parking lot, eating a late breakfast, and plotting to put the hurt on some guy claiming to be a seer.

Never mind that I'd only be digging a deeper hole for myself. That I was supposed to be in class. That I'd be grounded for the rest of my natural life, or worse.

There was nothing wrong with my father other than his drinking problems. Even if I could hear the man think.

I jumped out of the car.

Rude lunged after me, but he only caught a handful of sweatshirt, which I shrugged out of. The big guy bolted out of the vehicle after me. Running, for crying out loud. Why try to stop me?

I poured on the speed, picking it up to full throttle. I was faster than Rude and I had a head start. My sneakers skidded on the blacktop by the passenger side of the Suburban. I banged on the door with the flat of my hand.

Dad paused mid-bite, egg sandwich hanging out of his mouth. He met my gaze without a flash of recognition or surprise or welcome. There was nothing behind his eyes, as if he wasn't even there. As if he was empty.

And he had a gun on the seat beside him. My dad, who had never owned a gun in his life.

I backed up—straight into Rude. Who grabbed hold of me and swung me away from the open window. Took me down to the ground.

Rude's thoughts echoed in my skull. *Stay down.*

Rude thought my own father would fire on us. He thought Franklin Landon would shoot his own son.

But Dad didn't do anything like that. He gunned the engine to life and punched the gas. The rear of the Suburban fishtailed. The tires kicked a spray of asphalt pebbles into my face.

I shut my eyes tight—quick enough. But I couldn't turn away in time to keep the flying rocks from scoring my skin. I couldn't move. I could barely breathe with Rude on top of me.

"Off," I grunted.

"You okay?" the big guy asked, and pushed to his feet.

I gulped air. "No."

Rude extended a hand to help me up. I stared at it for a minute before I took it. I didn't want to know any of what I'd learned over the last couple of days. I didn't want to need help, but I did. I needed all the help I could get.

I brushed myself off. When I touched my face, my fingers came away bloody.

"It's not as bad as it looks," Rude said.

I narrowed my eyes.

He held up a hand in truce.

"I don't understand what just went down here," I said.

"Oscar can explain it," Rude said.

"Tell him to come explain it out here."

"You need to wash those cuts. We can do that inside."

"Later," I said. "I want answers. Right now."

CHAPTER 12

RUDE REACHED FOR HIS CELL. Before he could text, the door to the restaurant opened. Oscar jogged out, gauged the traffic, and crossed the road.

He looked bigger than I remembered from the other night. His biceps bulged inside the short sleeves of his white undershirt. No sweater. No coat. He hadn't taken the time to put one on. That should mean something, but I couldn't think what.

"Inside," Oscar said.

I shook my head. "I already told Rude no. Whatever it is, say it to me here."

Oscar took hold of my arm. "Those pseudo cops will be here any minute. Do you want to be out in the open for them to pick you up?"

"How would they know I'm here?"

"I'll tell you inside," Oscar said.

"Why would they pick me up?"

"We're not in school," Rude said. "We're truant. That's a human reason. No clue if they've got another one."

Shit.

"If they look like cops, no one will even look at them sideways when they shove you in the car," Rude said.

That got me moving.

The back room of the restaurant was warm enough to spring a sweat on my forehead. Oscar brought me a hot cocoa spiced with chili and cinnamon. I drank it all in one long swallow, burning my mouth. I gripped the empty mug with both hands, afraid to let it go. As if it was the only solid thing I had left to hold on to.

Maybe it was.

Oscar sat on one side of me, Rude on the other—flanking me as if they wanted to support me. Or keep me from running out the door.

"What's wrong with my father?" I asked. "Straight-up. No games. No 'go to this address before midnight' crap."

Oscar folded his hands and rested them on the tabletop. "He's been messing with powers he doesn't understand."

I met the man's gaze and saw only honesty. Exactly what I'd asked for.

Oscar spoke low. "Your mother died last October, didn't she?"

Tears welled in my eyes. I blinked them back. "Halloween."

"And your dad's been acting strange since that happened?"

"Wouldn't you?"

"I would," Oscar said.

"So what are you trying to say, man?"

"Your father's been trying to bring her back."

"That's impossible."

"It's not," Oscar said. "Not if the person in question died a mystical death. Not if you know what you're doing. Who to contact, both here and in the Faery realm. They watch over the dead."

After everything that'd happened the last few days, I could only take what he said at face value. "A drunk killed my mother."

"What if your father doesn't believe that?" Oscar asked.

But it happened the way the cops said it did. Confirmed by the coroner. "Who would tell him different?"

"I did," Oscar said.

I stared at him. "You? How would he even know who you are?"

"He sought me out. I'm not that hard to find." He gestured at me, seeming to mean that after all, if I could find him, how hard could it be?

But I'd had help. I turned to look at Rude, who'd been too quiet ever since we'd sat down. "Please tell me you didn't bring my dad here."

"It wasn't like that," Rude said. "Not exactly."

Dread touched a chilled finger to my heart. "Well then, how exactly was it?"

Rude stole a glance at Oscar. If he was looking for help from his teacher, he didn't get it.

"I felt bad for him," he said. "He needed something to hold on to."

I glanced at the mug I white-knuckled, then forced myself to set it down.

Rude went on. "I figured I could get him to talk to someone, and maybe he'd be able to be himself again."

"Be himself?" I asked.

"C'mon, dude—your life has radically sucked since your mom died, and he hasn't been a lot of help."

"He's trying."

"Trying isn't good enough," Rude said.

Well, there wasn't anything I could do about that, was there? I was doing the best I could, too. What if that wasn't enough?

"You'd know a lot about that," I said. "Seeing as your life's so perfect. Big house, big car, plenty of cash."

Rude held up a hand. "Stop right there, Kev."

"Why should I?"

"You sound like an asshole," Rude said.

I couldn't have cared less. "So what if I am one?"

Rude let the question hang long enough for me to hear how stupid I sounded, which only made me angrier.

"You're just pissed because I'm right," Rude said.

Maybe I was. "What did you tell him?" I asked Oscar.

"That it was possible his wife was carried off by the Wild Hunt. He never saw her body—never had to make an identification, no open casket at the funeral."

Because she'd been mangled too badly in the wreck.

And wait—that hunt thing—the name was just like the band that Rude had talked about. Just like the page Dad had been checking out online.

"He asked me how to know for sure," Oscar continued. "I sent him to the same place I sent the two of you last night—to the girl on the bus. I told him she would know what to do for him, if anything could be done."

I tried to imagine my dad going to see Simone. My stubborn, accounts-payable-clerk father. I just couldn't see it.

"Why did you do that?" I asked. "You should have known better."

My father wasn't the kind of guy who could handle that kind of reality shift. That would've been obvious to anyone with eyes.

"I didn't know," Oscar said. "I didn't know your dad. He was convinced. He believed utterly that his wife had not died. And he needed my help. Who was I not to give it to him?"

"So you were trying to be kind."

Oscar nodded.

Stupid. Sometimes helping someone like that was the *least* kind thing you could do. If Oscar had just said *No, you're wrong*, then…then my dad would have found another way to get what he wanted. And maybe the next person he went to for help wouldn't be a good guy.

I wanted to hate Oscar, but I couldn't bring myself to do it. Not yet.

"Why the girl on the bus? Why her in particular?"

"She's special," Oscar said. "She used to be a flesh-and-blood human girl. She was in the wrong place at the wrong time, out on Halloween night. She ran into the Hunt."

The Hunt. Again. "You want to fill in the blanks?"

Rude did. "The Wild Hunt rides the sky every year on Halloween. It's a procession of ghostly hunters led by the Faery King. Usually, they're hunting a woman. Otherwise, they take the souls of the newly dead with them to Faery. Sometimes they also take the souls of people unlucky enough to run into them, leaving their dead bodies behind."

"Busy fuckers," I said.

"Sometimes they kidnap living people, dude. That's what happened to our girl."

"The fae kidnapped her." I could only imagine how incredibly terrifying that would've been. And she'd been changed. Human to fae. "How'd she get the wings?"

"Someone stays in Faery long enough, they start to change," Oscar said. "Or the King or Queen does it because they want to. For her, it was both."

"How long was she there?" I asked.

"She's still there, Kev."

I thought about last night. About going to visit her. Just because the bus seemed to be anchored in our world didn't mean it was. It visited for a few hours, that was all.

"She's been in Faery seven years, Kev. She was twenty-four when they took her."

That would make her thirty-one now. "But she doesn't look that old."

"Time moves a lot more slowly there. There's no way to tell how old she is anymore," Oscar said.

"Why'd the Hunt take her?" I asked.

"The King," Oscar said. "He wanted her. Wanted the power of her voice. She still hangs on to hope that one day she'll be able to come back home, back to her life. But if it doesn't happen soon, she'll be too far changed to do it."

"But the wings—"

"Still flesh and blood," Rude said.

I remembered: the ripple of muscle and the course of blood.

Rude glanced down at the table. "Eventually, she'll just become light. She won't have a physical, human body at all. She'll lose that part of herself. It's her destiny, and there's no going back."

"How long does she have before that happens?"

"A hundred years," Rude said.

Jesus. What would that be like? To watch yourself change into something unrecognizable? To know it would be irreversible?

"Until that happens, she walks with a foot in both worlds—human and fae," Oscar said.

"How does she get free?" I asked.

Oscar leaned toward me. "Someone else must go to Faery in her place. Or she must be ransomed by a person with as great a talent as she possesses, a person who is willing to challenge the fae to a contest of art."

"Come again?"

"Her voice," Rude said. "She can make you feel any emotion she wants."

That didn't sound like such a big deal. "All music does that if it's good."

"Not like this, Kev. She can make you love her—or want to kill the guy standing next to you. One note is all it takes."

I'd have to take Rude's word for it. If I could ever trust him again. How could Rude not have told me all of this?

I wouldn't have believed a word of it before yesterday.

"Someone with more talent than that would have to fight for her and win, dude."

That was screwed up. And impossible. Which meant she'd never be free.

The more I knew, the more I wanted to run screaming down the street with my hair on fire.

I took a deep breath and blew it out slowly. Then another. And then another after that. All that oxygen started to clear my head and slow my heartbeat. My chest hurt. I pressed the heel of my hand to the ache before I understood that the pain was for Simone. For my dad. For all of us.

One thing at a time.

I spoke softly. "So you two sent my father to the Super Singer Bus Girl because she would be able to tell if my mom was kidnapped the same way she was."

Rude tapped a finger on the table. Didn't answer.

"And you thought he could help her as much as she might be able to help him."

"More or less," Rude said.

"He's not talented."

"He loves with his whole heart and soul," Oscar said. "That's something. To some people, that's everything."

I could get with that explanation, as far as it went. "Did he try to help her?"

Oscar nodded. "That's what broke him, we think."

"You *think*? All this woo-woo you claim to know, and you're not sure?"

Oscar didn't have an answer for that. Silence settled over the room, punctuated by the serious clanging of pots and pans and shouted instructions in the kitchen.

"What exactly does 'broken' mean?" I asked.

"There's a part of him that's stuck in Faery. He's half-here, half-there. Half of himself."

"Like the bus girl."

"No. It's much worse," Oscar said.

I opened my mouth to ask why.

Oscar interrupted. "I don't know, Kevin."

The worst thought slipped into my mind. "Could he die?"

Oscar took his time answering. Which worried me worse.

"It's possible," the seer said. "Probable, even. You can't walk around like that forever. His spirit will want to reunite itself into one whole. It will eventually do that, in Faery."

"Not here?"

"It's never happened that way before that I know of." Oscar paused. "When his spirit reunites in Faery, his body will die here."

I couldn't—wouldn't—wrap my mind around that. A yawning hole opened up in my gut. My mom had been gone eleven months, twenty-five days, nine hours. And now my dad?

I flattened my palms on the tabletop. "How long does he have?"

Oscar and Rude passed a glance. As if they'd had this conversation before without me.

I balled my hands into fists. "Tell me."

"A week at the outside," Oscar said.

Not much time. Not enough time.

I would not let this thing go down without doing everything in my power—and Oscar's, and Rude's, and whoever-the-hell-else's—to stop it.

CHAPTER 13

OSCAR LOOKED AT ME differently than he had up until then. I couldn't say how it was different, just that it made me feel bigger, like I could actually help my dad—like I had a chance. But I also felt in way over my head. Oscar expected something of me that I might not be able to deliver. What would happen if I couldn't? I felt as if my head and my heart would explode with the weight of it.

The postered walls and concrete floor seemed to spin around us. The clang of pots and sharp bark of voices from the kitchen faded, as if they existed in another dimension. I couldn't smell the spices and comforting scents of the food as it cooked. I could only smell my own fear, and it stank of musk and sweat.

I met Rude's gaze. He looked as uncomfortable as I felt.

"She's the key. The girl on the bus," Oscar said.

Simone. "Have you asked her version of what happened with my dad?"

"She had nothing to say. I'm no one to her. However, from what Rude told me of your time with her last night, she'll help you."

Rude told his teacher about what happened between Simone and me? I wasn't even sure what had happened, and Rude had already shared it with Oscar. I glared at Rude. He winced.

Oscar snapped his fingers. "Enough. You don't get to keep secrets. You don't get to have private moments, not until this is over. You understand?"

The words penetrated my skull. I heard. I understood. My feelings didn't matter. All that mattered was saving lives. My dad's. And not just his—Simone's.

"Will she be in the same place tonight, same time?" I asked.

"She's there every night," Oscar said. "Between midnight and dawn. But not always until dawn."

"No other way to contact her sooner?"

"There's only the name she gave you. You shouldn't use it unless it's an emergency."

"This isn't one?" Obviously, Oscar didn't understand the meaning of word.

"There are degrees," Oscar said.

"You mean this could get worse?"

Oscar nodded. "You could sit here all afternoon and fail to turn in your English paper. You need that grade to pass the class."

To get my scholarship. "How do you know that?"

"Seer," Oscar said.

"I'll send you back to school with a couple of burritos. You do your job there," Oscar said. "And whatever you do after that, don't go home."

I looked from Oscar to Rude and back again. "What are you talking about?"

"It's not safe, Kevin," Oscar said.

"My dad wouldn't hurt me." Even though Dad hadn't recognized me. Even though there'd been a gun on the seat.

"There's no way to know what he'll do, Kevin," Oscar said.

"I thought you were a seer."

"People are hard to predict," Oscar said. "Choices can turn on a dime. If they don't have a clue what they're about to do, how could I?"

Was that a real reason? Or did Oscar know something he wasn't saying? "You would come clean if you saw something, no matter how bad it was. Right?"

Oscar held my gaze without saying a word. After a while, it started to feel like a stare-down. What could Oscar prove with that? It wasn't *his* father running around out there half-alive.

Oscar sighed. "I'll promise you that if you want. You may hate me for it."

"I've got no problem with that."

"Nice to know." The seer cracked a sad smile. "You still can't go home."

But I belonged at home. "No."

"Dude, what if you're wrong about your dad?" Rude asked.

Would my father hurt me? Kill me in my sleep? Dad had never raised a hand to me—well, once, under the worst circumstances. Usually, when he got upset, he withdrew. Until today, I'd never really thought about him in the same neighborhood as violence.

He was angry with Oscar. He wanted revenge. I could understand that. What I didn't get was why he watched and waited. If Dad had known Oscar as long as Oscar said, then he knew when Oscar would be at the restaurant, when he arrived and when he left. He probably knew where Oscar lived and the places he liked to go.

"Why hasn't he shot you yet?" I asked.

Oscar took his time answering. "He thinks he can use me as a bargaining chip with the King of Faery. I'm the ransom he plans to pay for your mother. Makes no sense, because the Faery King doesn't want me for anything. No convincing your father of that, though."

So Dad was watching and waiting for the right moment to kidnap Oscar. He hadn't tried yet because Oscar could see him coming, literally. That was one piece of the unbelievable puzzle. What about the rest?

"And the cops, the ones who are after me? What are they, really?"

"They belong to the Faery King. They're two of his agents in this world."

Meaning there were more where they came from. And meaning they weren't police. My gut feeling had been right. Rude had been right. And Rude wouldn't look at me.

"So they can't touch me," I said to Oscar. "They can't arrest me. I'm not being framed for murder."

Oscar shook his head. "You won't be arrested, but you are being framed in every way that matters. Hasn't everyone at school heard a rumor that you knew the dead girl, that you had something to do with her murder?"

The rumor had spread like wildfire.

"They're busy screwing up your life as much as possible right now," Oscar said. "Making sure you have nothing left—nobody to turn to, no one who'll miss you much when he takes you."

He. The Faery King. "Takes me?"

"To Faery, dude."

"On Halloween night," Oscar added. "When the Hunt rides the sky."

Like he'd taken Simone. "What the hell does he want with me?"

Oscar shrugged. "Your new gift?"

"My curse, you mean. And you're asking, so that means you don't know."

"I'm ninety-five percent sure," Oscar said.

With five percent uncertainty and a who-knows-what margin of error. A lot of help, this guy. Tell me that I was in life-or-death kind of danger without giving me an out. The news—on top of hearing about Dad—the overwhelm was like a tidal wave bearing down on me.

I sucked in a breath to keep from drowning in the feeling. "What can I do?"

"Don't go out on Halloween," Oscar said. "Hide. It's the only thing that might save you."

Might. Meaning maybe. I needed more than maybes.

I heard myself speak, but my voice sounded like the sounds flowing from the kitchen—far away. "I have a date."

I hoped I still had one.

"Take a rain check. If you're in hiding, the King and his Hunt might not be able to find you. If they can't find you, they can't take you."

"That's way too simple. If that's all there is to it, how come everybody in the Hunt's crosshairs doesn't just do that?"

"Stupidity or ignorance," Oscar said. "If you're taken, you'll know which one of those to chalk it up to."

Wow. "Have you always been a douchebag?"

"You said you wanted to hear the straight-up truth. I'm giving it to you."

Rude jumped in. "Let me have your key, dude. I can get your stuff when your dad's not home. Bring it to you at school."

Where exactly was I supposed to go?

I met Rude's gaze. "You gonna put me up?"

"I can make my parents forget little things, dude. You're something else."

"Oh yeah, sure."

"Really," Rude said.

I turned to Oscar. "What about you?"

"I don't have an open house," Oscar said.

"You're supposed to help me," I said. "And you—*dude*—you're supposed to be my friend. You can't think of anything? I mean, it's not like Amy's parents are gonna want me surfing on their couch. It's not like I can go stay with Scott, is it?"

Rude sighed. "I'll figure something out."

"Thanks for making me feel like I'm a problem."

"I didn't mean it that way, dude."

I pressed the heels of my hands against my eyes until I saw spots. How had things gotten to this point? And how did we fix it? Zero in: what could I do to fix it?

I couldn't run and hide while people I cared about were in danger. I refused to be that guy.

Oscar frowned. "Be careful, Kevin. If you're going to go home, then pay attention. If you start to hear your father think, get out. Something will be about to go down. Whatever it is, you won't be able to stop it."

Maybe Oscar was right. Maybe he was wrong. All I knew was that we were talking about how unpredictable people were. How things could change on a dime—or a split-second decision. If that was true, then we weren't talking about fate or destiny. We were talking about choices, and I had them.

By the time Rude and I walked into the remains of the stormy morning, into the parking lot where I'd come face-to-face with my dad in worse trouble than I could've ever imagined, I could only think about how to help him. How to save his life.

How to save us all.

CHAPTER 14

W E PARKED OUT BACK of the school and ate lunch in the car as the sun emerged from the clouds, not talking about what happened, for which I felt profoundly thankful.

A few days ago, I'd have sat shotgun and bitched about little things. A bad day would have been if I'd had a pop quiz and didn't have all the material down enough to get an A, or if the gym coach made us do pull-ups. Now that kind of stuff seemed far away and small.

Rude took his last bite of beans and cheese and tortilla, then crumpled the foil wrapper. "You have time to catch up with me before you go home, dude?"

I had gym, study hall, English. How was I supposed to act normal through all of that? Then again, no one expected me to act normal anymore. "Not much time. My dad's picking me up right after."

Rude tossed the foil into the back seat. "You gonna reconsider going home?"

"No."

"I'm around if you need me."

Rude meant it, and that meant a lot. "Thanks, man."

"Don't mention it," Rude said. "I'll be at the front door, main building after the last bell—on the inside, so your dad doesn't see us. If you can stop, I might have something important for you."

"Can you be a little more vague about that?"

"If I was sure I'd have it, I'd be Captain Obvious."

"Funny, man."

I'd never really understood the concept of gallows humor before. Now, it felt like all I had.

The lunch bell rang and the schoolyard began to fill with bodies. We slipped on our shades, got out, and headed over.

I found Amy on the second floor, at her locker. I cleared my throat as she backed up to shut the door. She leaned into me and didn't make a move to break contact, or even glance over her shoulder. She spoke low, so close to my ear, I could feel the warmth of her breath.

"Where'd you go this morning?"

For one gut-churning second, she reminded me of Simone. The girl I wanted versus the girl who, according to Rude, wanted me. Human versus fae.

If I was in danger, was I putting the people—the innocent, unknowing people—around me in danger, too? Could Amy get hurt?

I wouldn't allow that to happen.

"Rude had an errand to run," I said. "He needed me to go with."

Not strictly a lie, although it gave the truth an awful wide berth. It rolled off my tongue too easily. I didn't want to lie to her, but better to lie if it would keep her safe.

She turned a little so she could see my face.

I tried to smooth my expression. To be cool.

"You never skip school, Kevin."

"It's not a new habit. Just a one-time deal."

"You're not gonna tell me where you went, are you?" she asked.

I winked. "Plausible deniability."

"And last night?"

"I had a fight with my dad." More untruth. Even if we *had* fought this morning.

"You could've just said so before."

"Sorry."

Her face softened. "Britt said some shit about you."

"I figured from your message."

"I know you, Kevin. I know the gossip isn't true."

"You know her, too. She's your friend."

She shrugged. "Maybe she is. Maybe I'm figuring out that the word 'friend' means different things to different people."

"After the last couple of days, I know a lot about that."

She shifted her weight from one foot to the other, then changed the subject. "You missed some important stuff in Stat today. It'll be on the test, but it's not in the book."

Once upon a time, that would've been of vital importance. Now, I could barely get worked up. My voice reflected the unnatural calm I felt. "Can I borrow your notes?"

"Yeah. Or I could come over and help you study tonight."

Any night but tonight. "I'd be stupid not to take you up on that."

"You're not stupid." She pressed closer to me.

"I can't tonight."

"Really?"

"It's embarrassing," I said. "Give me a couple of days."

The crisis would be over by then, one way or another. I hoped.

I wrapped my arms around her, one around her waist and the other a little higher, the top of my hand brushing the bottom of her breast through her lace camisole. I could feel her heart race. My own heartbeat sped up, and all the blood rushed away from my brain, all of it headed south.

I wouldn't have minded if we'd been anywhere except the hall. I did *not* want to have a boner for all the world to see.

She placed a hand behind my neck and pulled me in closer, brushing her lips against mine. She tasted sweet, and the promise in her kiss made me forget about the world entirely. My mind bent to all the private nooks and empty rooms close by. Somewhere we could. No one else around—

And the bell rang.

She pulled away, her jade eyes clouded with the same lust and pique I felt. "Only two more days 'til Halloween."

The date. The one I was too grounded to take her on and the one my dad might not live to see. The night the Faery King might take me. All I wanted to do was be with her.

"Lucky me," I said.

"There's a party at Zoe's. Costumes and everything."

Costumes? Could be cool. Could be lame. But at Zoe's? Would Zoe even let a freak like me through the door?

How could I possibly be thinking about that when I had earth-shattering, life-altering shit to figure out?

Amy waved. I watched her walk off to class until she blended in with the rest of the crowd in the hall. I shook my head to clear it. I had, like, two minutes to get downstairs and to the other side of the school to make Gym. Which I did, barely. I suffered through it (no pull-ups, thank God), and through study hall.

I turned in my Grendel-the-Outcast treatise at the start of last period, and opened my copy of *Beowulf* to the announced unintelligible page printed in Middle English. The smell of the old paper, dust embedded in its pores, made me want to sneeze.

At the front of the room, Mrs. Cahill warbled on and on about the Value of the Unusual. She wore her red dress with the tiny white polka dots—looking at it always gave me a headache.

Ashley Benning, she of the brown nose and the front row, got tapped to read aloud first. All I could see of her was the back of her gray turtleneck and her mass of brown curls pulled back with a clip. She had one of those voices where everything she said might as well have gone down a well, so I couldn't make out any particular word, just the choppy cadence. Mrs. Cahill stopped her every sentence or two to explain a point or to write something on the blackboard in a furious scrape of chalk.

I tamped it all down to a dull roar. I couldn't have focused if I'd wanted to, since it took all of my brain power to count the number of minutes until the bell.

I couldn't stop thinking about Amy and the way her body felt against mine, the way she tasted. I also couldn't stop thinking about my dad, and Simone, and why a Faery King I'd never met wanted to screw up my life and steal me away.

My new power, as Oscar put it, blew. I didn't want it. I hadn't asked for it. I didn't know why it'd suddenly chosen me, or how to make it go away. I could see how knowing a deadly danger was close was valuable. I had to make it work for me, and not passively.

Having thoughts pop into my head like they had so far was great, but I hadn't been trying to do anything dangerous any of those times. Things had happened to me. I hadn't been trying to make things happen.

That was about to change.

I caught sight of a shadow from the corner of my eye and snapped to attention just as Mrs. Cahill loomed over me, glaring. She tapped her manicured nails on the hardcover back of the book she held.

"Having some difficulty joining us today, Mr. Landon?"

The rest of the class snickered, especially Ashley Benning. Ha, ha, ha.

"Sorry," I said.

She bent over my desk and gazed at me for a moment with sympathy that, thank God, no one else saw. I felt bone-tired of seeing that look and the gleeful, hungry faces of everyone else in the room.

What freaky thing was I doing now? What juicy gossip could they pass on to their friends?

I wished I'd stayed out of school the whole day. Or all week. Long enough for someone else to fuck up bad enough to divert all the attention from me.

I could excuse myself now. Plead sickness. It would be the truth—I could feel nausea coming on. Mrs. Cahill would let me go, but she'd know why I asked. And maybe half the class would guess.

I wasn't a coward. I wouldn't run away. If I could face down a Faery King, I could deal with all of these motherfuckers.

The moment passed. Mrs. Cahill pointed at my book. "Please read the next three paragraphs, Kevin."

I mutilated the Middle English to her satisfaction. When she finally turned her back, I stole a glance at the clock.

She spoke without looking at me. "The bell will ring when it's time to go, Mr. Landon."

Woman had eyes in the back of her head. "Yes, ma'am."

"Continue reading."

I did, painfully. Until a knock sounded on the door.

Mr. Nance, the counselor, poked his head inside. "I need Kevin."

Mrs. Cahill grinned. "Saving him from a fate worse than death?"

"I'm afraid not."

CHAPTER 15

I STARTED TO get up from the desk.

"Bring your stuff," Mr. Nance said.

Not a good sign. What had I done wrong? No—what had I done to get caught? And wouldn't someone from the principal's office have come to get me if this was about the missed classes?

I shoved my book into my backpack and followed Mr. Nance to his office. As hard as I tried, I couldn't get a vibe from the guy. Nance didn't say a word, and he didn't glance back at me.

The click of the counselor's dress shoes and the squeak of my sneakers on the tile echoed in the hall, punctuated by stray bits of lecture from the few open-door classrooms we passed. The counselor waved at the secretary in the front office, a lady who wore a navy suit and peered at Nance and me through her rhinestone-encrusted bifocals as if we were curiosities. You know, like zoo animals.

Nance's office looked the same as it had the one and only time I'd been inside. Neat stacks of papers all over the desk and credenza, in no order I could figure, with an arm's length of clean space in the center. Once, I'd heard that Nance had a secret filing system so no one could sneak a peek at the student records, which seemed paranoid and delusional.

The bookcase hadn't been dusted in a thousand years. A half-dead ivy sat on top, trailers with as many brown as green leaves hanging down over the sides of the shelves. There was exactly one piece of art, on the back wall: an oil painting of a bunch of guys riding horses through the air, in formation like a flock of geese. All of them wore crowns. The dude at the head of the line shone as if he had a star in his chest. The brass plaque on the frame read *The Wild Hunt*.

All the spit in my mouth dried up.

The same picture I'd seen on my father's computer the night of the party. The same Wild Hunt that would come after me. What were the odds this was a coincidence? Maybe I'd believed in those at some point, but now I felt as if the walls were closing in.

Mr. Nance shut the door and cocked his head at one of the red vinyl guest chairs. I sat, not just because he wanted me to, but because my legs threatened to give out.

"We couldn't get ahold of your father this morning when we called to find out why you weren't in class," Nance said.

No kidding.

"So I'll need a note from you."

Note. The kind your parents sent to school with you to excuse an absence.

"Why are you asking?"

"I'm not sure I understand the question, Kevin."

"Let me rephrase. Why are *you* asking?"

Mr. Nance sat down behind his desk and rested his forearms on the clean space, steepling his fingers. "Interesting."

"What's interesting?"

"You're not denying that you skipped class."

I said nothing.

He nodded. "We got a call from an officer bright and early this morning. He told us what happened over the weekend, that you are a —how did they say it?—a person of interest in their investigation. The staff was informed."

A person of interest? Informed? The King had really upped the ante. It wouldn't matter whether someone else did something bigger and stupider. Nothing was going to eclipse this. Not now, and maybe not ever. I held my breath.

"My main concern, Kevin, is that this might affect your ability to get the scholarship you need for college."

No matter that I hadn't been actually accused of anything. No matter that the whole thing had been trumped up. Oscar had warned me. Oscar was right.

Mr. Nance took my silence as evidence that I was stunned. I was— just not the way he thought.

"They will do background checks," he said. "And when they do, they may find out about this incident. They may decline to extend an offer. There are other candidates vying for the same money who don't have a murder hanging over them."

For the first time, I understood that people hadn't been staring at me or talking about me like I was some freak because they heard I had something to do with a dead girl. They were wondering if I'd actually done it. If I'd killed her.

The nausea bloomed full force. "Holy shit."

"Just so. I could just patronize you like any other adult in this office might do. I could speak some platitude about how everything will be all right and send you back to class. My eyes would brim with sympathy, like Mrs. Cahill's. How would that be?"

"How did you know Mrs. Cah—"

"Please, Kevin. A person would have to be willfully blind to miss her fakery. She behaves that way with everyone. Didn't you know?"

I hadn't thought much about it. I'd kept my head down. Studied hard. All I'd wanted was a ticket out of my life and the keys to a new one. Look where I'd ended up.

I didn't owe Mr. Nance anything. Not an apology for skipping class. Not an explanation for what had happened to me since the fateful moment I'd heard Scott's drunken thoughts skittering through my gray matter. But I needed to say something.

"I didn't do it."

Four words that meant everything to me right now. I didn't care what, if anything, they meant to Nance.

The counselor nodded as if he'd expected me to say them. "I'll still need that note."

"When?"

"Now."

"How about tomorrow morning, first thing?" That would give me a chance to write up something. Forge my dad's signature.

"No."

"I was sick."

Mr. Nance sighed. "You know, I met your father once. At the open house last year."

There had been a spaghetti supper and parent-teacher conferences. Dad had been drunk.

"He's not going to produce an excuse for you," Nance said. "It's probably the last thing on his mind."

The counselor had to know what I planned to do. And that was a problem from which I had no exit.

Mr. Nance pulled a sheet of notebook paper from his drawer and wrote. I read it upside down.

To Whom It May Concern:

Kevin was unable to attend all of his classes on Tuesday morning, October 28th, because of a bout of food poisoning.

Franklin Landon

"Good enough?" Mr. Nance asked.

To get him fired, sure. "Why are you helping me?"

"Because, once upon a time, I was just like you."

I sincerely doubted that. "What's the catch?"

"That you stay on the straight-and-narrow, get into a good college, go there, and graduate," Mr. Nance said. "Do you think you can do that?"

What were the odds? "I hope so."

"Don't hope, Kevin. Do it."

I nodded.

"I'm going to send this note to admin. It'll go in your file. They won't try to contact your father again."

A good thing. "Thanks, Mr. Nance."

"You're welcome. You also have my permission to skip the last ten minutes of Mrs. Cahill's class." Mr. Nance shuffled the papers on his desk. Our session was over.

I stood up, legs steadier than I expected. "How come you trust me?"

Mr. Nance met my gaze. "Like I said, I was just like you. My father...well, my father never won any awards for parent of the year."

I tried not to blanch at that. I might resent the hell out of my dad for the ways in which he'd abandoned me, but right now worry took precedence. Worry that he might die. That even if I figured out a way to help him, he might never be the same.

No matter how bad it had been or would get, I loved him.

Mr. Nance meant well. He showed his sympathy differently than Mrs. Cahill, but deep down it felt the same to me. Humiliating.

I forced myself to say something polite. "Thank you again, Mr. Nance."

"You try hard, Kevin. You do your best. You'll make it. You'll get to college."

"Yes, sir."

"Just so," Mr. Nance said. "Remember one thing, Kevin. If you have any more problems, my door is always open. Any kind of problems, no matter how unusual."

I stared at him. Did he know? How could he—

The door to the office swung open. The girl from the party, the blond with the eyebrow ring—it had to be the same girl—marched in like she owned the place. Her eyes were red, white, and hazel, like she'd been crying.

She sounded stopped up when she spoke. "They did it again, Mr. Nance. Fuckers."

"Just so," Nance said, by way of agreement.

I looked from one to the other. The girl had the counselor's full attention, and she his.

Time to go. I couldn't help overhearing a few words as I slipped out.

"Language, Ms. Kinsey. What did you do in retaliation?"

"Egged their lockers," she said. "From the inside."

"And how did you do that?" Mr. Nance asked.

I wanted to know, too.

Kinsey shrugged. "Magic."

Magic was no joking matter. I scowled at her back and went in search of Rude.

CHAPTER 16

RUDE WAS WHERE he'd promised to be—at the front doors—cradling a brown paper sack close to his body to protect it from the exiting hordes. With the doors opening and closing so much, the outdoor chill seeped in and the temperature where we stood dropped a good five degrees inside a couple of minutes. A cold front had blown in while we'd been in class.

It didn't hold a candle to the icy fear that had settled into my gut. Out there on the curb, my dad would be waiting.

I nodded at the lunch sack. "That the something important?"

"It is. I had to skip study hall to make it." Rude handed it over.

The sack felt heavier than it looked. I started to open it, but stopped once I caught the caution on Rude's face.

"Not yet, dude. Not until I tell you what's in there and what it's for," Rude said. "I know I said before that I'm around if you need me, but that's not exactly true tonight. And tonight might be crucial."

"Thank you, Captain Obvious."

Rude chuckled. It was a tired laugh. "I'll be with Oscar."

"Paying the price?"

"I'll be okay, if you're wondering. I'll just be incommunicado for a few hours."

"C'mon, man. Why won't you tell me?"

"In the hall with a thousand eavesdroppers? I'll call you when I'm home."

I guessed I could live with that. "So what's the big surprise in the bag?"

"It's a charm, like the one I told you about, the one Oscar taught me."

I peered into the bag and saw a large, polished river rock, the same kind as lined the yard where Rude hung out and smoked. No wonder the thing felt heavy.

"I didn't think it would be a thing," I said. "The charm, I mean. I thought it would be something you say."

"That's an incantation, dude. A whole other animal."

Whatever. Either one equaled magic. "So what do I do with this? Bash my dad over the head with it if he gets out of hand?"

Rude rolled his eyes. "Hold it in your hand and think at it."

"Think at it?" He had to be kidding.

Apparently not. "*Forget*, that's what you think. As in, your dad will forget whatever you need him to. It'll set off the charm, which will give you some time to get the hell outta Dodge if you need to."

"Okay—understood." I shrugged out of my backpack and unzipped the small, front pocket.

Rude shook his head. "Slip it in your pocket, dude. Keep it on you. That way you'll have it if you need it, and it won't be on the other side of the house."

I bowed to the logic. The thing made a nice bulge in my pants that I could just cover with my sweatshirt. "I sure hope my dad doesn't ask me if there's a sock in my pocket or if I'm just happy to see him."

"If he does, use your sarcasm superpowers," Rude said. "Leave no trace, remember?"

"I do." I stretched out a hand.

Rude clasped it, pulled me in, and thumped me on the back. "Do me a favor tonight and don't go out."

"First it's 'don't go home'. Now it's 'don't go out'. Which is it?"

"If you're going investigating, I want to go with you. You need someone to watch your back."

Unless I went to see Simone. I could do that safely enough. Although my definition of "safe" had changed a bit.

"See you tomorrow, but talk to you later, dude."

"Yeah," I said. "Later. Thanks."

Nothing to do now except step out into the cold. The afternoon light had faded with the arrival of the front, leaving the sky mostly gray except for a spot on the horizon where the sun streamed through at just the right angle to half-blind me. Didn't stop me from bull's-eyeing the Suburban at the curb, though.

The dad who sat behind the wheel had done a one-eighty since the west-side parking lot. Either that, or he had to be a completely different guy. He didn't seem broken at all.

Because he said, "Hi, Kev. How was your day?"

He didn't sound the least bit annoyed at feeling like he had to pick me up from school, or embarrassed or pissed that I'd seen him in a parking lot with a gun, stalking a faery seer in order to kidnap him. He also sounded stone cold sober.

How was my day? "Like a funhouse mirror, Dad."

"That bad?"

"It's high school," I said.

"Well, get in and I'll take you away from it."

I hesitated for a heartbeat, watching for any signs of homicidal weirdness—and listening for thoughts. Nada. Deeper wrinkles than usual framed Dad's eyes, which upon closer inspection had a wild look about them. Wild, and trapped.

I held my breath while I climbed in, and released it slow. No gun on the seat. No sudden movements. It would be okay. Please, let it be okay.

Dad put the vehicle in gear and pulled out into traffic.

"How was your day, Dad?" A harmless question. A normal question.

"Good. I finally got a lead on a project I've been working on for a long time."

Definitely good—if it was true. "What project is it?"

"A dispute with a client. They're behind six months on our invoices, but they wouldn't pay until we made some adjustments, and the system wouldn't let us make the required changes. But now I think we've got it licked."

Usually, when Dad spoke accounting-ese, it bored me to death. Not this time.

"You reschedule your Halloween date?" he asked.

For a hot minute, I considered using the lucky charm in my pocket to undo the grounding. But that was as far as I got. What if something worse happened?

What had Rude said I should use as my alternative weapon? *Sarcasm, it is.* "Throw a brick at me, why don't you?"

"Just because we're having a friendly conversation doesn't mean you're not still grounded," Dad said. "It just means I'm tired of fighting, tired of hard words. If I have to be the grounder and you have to be the groundee, at least we can be civil to each other and get through this as painlessly as possible."

"Easy for you to say, Dad."

"But not for me to do."

Whoa. "Is this where you tell me it's harder for you than it is for me? Are you canceling a date for Friday night?"

"Did you?"

"What?"

"Cancel it."

"Not yet," I said.

"Well, get to it, son."

I glared out the window.

Dad sighed. "I want us to go home and have a good dinner. Then you'll go to your room and do your homework."

It went down just like that. Dad chilled in the living room while I did all my usual chores and cooking. After dinner, I struggled with Chemistry homework, realizing with real horror that I didn't understand it at all. That it would never be easy like Biology, which I'd aced, no problem. Even if I lived through the next couple of days, I was doomed. And if I didn't figure out the homework, so was my grade.

At bedtime, Dad locked himself in his room with a beer and whatever game he could find on ESPN. I gave up on Chem. I had some serious decisions to make.

Use the charm to un-ground myself—and save my date with Amy—or continue to keep it on standby, just in case. After all, the night was still young and until I got the all-clear from Rude, I had no other backup.

If I kept it in reserve and nothing happened, I could use it before I left for school tomorrow to do the deed and make my plans for Friday night.

In the meantime, did I go out or stay in?

If Simone held the key to solving Dad's problems, I had to see her. Sooner rather than later. And if I got caught? I still had the charm.

Seemed like I had all angles covered. I thought it through a second time, just to make sure. Then I set the timer on my desk lamp and went out the window because maybe last time it'd been my going out the front door that clued in my dad. I didn't leave another note. No point.

The night smelled like fallen leaves and damp earth. Those had been good smells—favorite scents—before Mom died. I breathed them in, trying to remember good things. Trying to convince myself that I could go back to a time when nothing felt complicated. When I could count on the world to play mostly fair.

That had been an illusion. Just like safety was an illusion.

The world didn't owe me anything. It'd made that clear as day, plain as the sun rising every morning in the east.

Tonight was a new beginning. If I had to live with the power to hear thoughts and understand mortal danger, then I was going to damn well act like I had power.

Not the power to steal Dad's car, though. Thieving the Suburban was out of the question. No way could I get it out of the garage and down the drive without making a ton of racket.

I rode my bike downtown, taking my life into my own hands with not one but two close calls involving screeching tires. All that in spite of having a decent reflective windbreaker and two blinking red safety lights plastered to my back and the back of the bike. Houston streets? Not made for the cycling.

I couldn't even relax once I hopped onto the trail along Buffalo Bayou. Too many shadows among the oaks and pines and magnolias and crepe myrtle. Water flowed low and easy at the bottom of the slope to my left, its glassy surface occasionally rippled by fish or fallen branches or who knew what else.

I dodged a couple of late-night joggers on the trail, and once I got closer to the skyscrapers, houseless people. A handful of them had set up camp under an overpass, backlit tonight by a construction crew building a footbridge support with the help of a couple of klieg lights and a bunch of orange-and-white barrels to warn off late-night drivers.

The houseless folks stared at me as I rode past. I tried on a smile, feeling stupid. I'd never wondered much about why they lived outdoors or what kind of raw deal life had handed them. I hated that it took my own life going over the edge for me to notice and think.

Magic had fucked up my life. Maybe it had fucked up theirs. Or maybe it'd been something else. The world—no, people—had let all this happen. The world—and people—needed fixing.

I carried that with me all the way to the alley, where I found the school bus in the exact same place as last night, just like Oscar promised. But Simone? Not home.

I knocked on the bus door. I tried to jimmy it open. I even sang it a song and felt like a weirdo the whole time as I belted out "Margaritaville." If a guy sang one of his dad's fav tunes in an alley and no one made a video to upload to the Internet, the guy could pretend it never happened. Right?

I sighed and checked my watch. It'd taken me a long time to ride out here. Just a little under an hour before the clock struck midnight. Simone should be there, but she wasn't.

What to do? Turn around and ride home? Looking around seemed like the best option. Provided I didn't run into any other interested parties, like the Faery King's pet policemen.

If I were Simone, where would I go?

Where would I go if I were a singer who'd lost her whole life? I'd go where the music was.

CHAPTER 17

I HEADED TOWARD the downtown clubs because they were closest—jazz bars and restaurants tucked into the skirts of high-rise lofts and empty office buildings. I found one basement dance club with bumping beats and not a lot of takers on a Tuesday night. Nothing rock-n-roll-forever down there. Too bourgie.

I turned east and went under the highway to check out the next likely place, a club called Phantom. Bound to be at least two bands playing in that half-finished warehouse. The right kinds of bands. Bass with a sex-you-up groove. Drums of thunder. Wailing guitar solos.

Street parking had filled blocks away, the tiny lot outside the club was packed to max. I chained my bike on the rack outside and said a small prayer that it'd still be there when I got back. I stepped inside the ground floor, immediately and painfully deafened.

The crash of music reverbed off the concrete floor and walls, making it impossible for me to hear the bouncer, who made it clear with blunt sign language that I wouldn't get in without handing over ID and the ten-dollar cover. Fake ID, no problem. Money might've been if I hadn't had twenty left over in my wallet after the last grocery run. Better to be thrifty. Better to save what I could in case I needed it.

I made my way deeper into the club. Heat poured from overhead vents. It dried out my throat and made me cough. Puddles of spilled beer slicked the floor. I watched where I walked and tried not to go down. I'd had enough humiliation for one day, please and thanks.

People clotted in small groups in the big open space that served as a lobby, red plastic cups in hand. Some of them congregated around the staircase in the middle of the room. Most of the traffic flowed up to the second floor.

The color of the night? Black. As in black clothes, black nails, black lips and eyes. The girls posed in stilettos and jeans and skirts so tight, it would be a miracle if any of them could sit down.

The guys wore T-shirts, some of them from old concerts, but most brand-new and bought from the card table in the corner. The shirts were multiple choice, with model tees duct-taped to the wall behind the dude minding the store.

The banner over the makeshift stand said BROKEN in three-foot Goth lettering. That got my attention. So did the picture of the band on the number 3 shirt—black, of course, with long sleeves.

Front and center? A nicely-rendered silver ink version of Simone. Ten bucks, which was all the cash I had left.

I got into line to buy one. When I got to the front, I pointed to the shirt I wanted and paid the man, who sported a leather bracelet emblazoned with the name MARCUS.

I leaned in close and yelled to be heard. "She's amazing!"

"Yeah," Marcus said. "She's the shit. Too bad she doesn't show up as often as she used to. When she does, though—man, she does it for me. Know what I mean?"

I didn't. Not in the same way the guy meant. "She here tonight?"

"She's been on upstairs for a half hour already. You just getting here?"

I nodded.

"Too bad, man. Better hurry or you'll miss the rest of the show."

If the heat had been uncomfortable downstairs, upstairs was explosively hot. Doors were propped open to the balcony to let some of the warm air out and gusts of chill in, along with a heaping helping of fumes from the smokers huddled out there. The stench helped cover over the equally unwelcome smell of thirty different kinds of cologne mixed with sweat and body odor.

I could still only hear the downstairs band. Not one note from Broken. The interior doors were closed, no clue which set I should go through to find them until a couple of the smokers came back in and headed around the corner and through a set of double doors.

I stripped off my windbreaker and tied it around my waist, and slipped on my new tee over the one I wore before I followed them in, joining a line that snaked around tables and bar stools. People were returning to their seats and taking spots along the walls. There'd been an intermission, and the band was about to come back on.

The woman in front of me turned off her cell phone. I followed suit. Just in time, too.

The band climbed onto the riser at the front of the room. The bassist and the guitarist picked up their instruments. The drummer sat down behind his kit. They looked like I'd felt when Rude and I woke up in the street last night—as if they'd had cartoon anvils dropped on their heads. And they glowed around the edges with the same magic I'd experienced on the bus with Simone. I could see it, and I'd bet the rest of the crowd could at least feel it.

Then the drummer counted off. The band began to play, a hypnotic wall of sound.

Simone took the stage, floating up the steps, floating on the groove. She had on a different dress than she'd worn last night, deep crimson of fresh blood with a ripped hem short enough to show off her long legs and delicate, bare feet. She wore a circlet of black roses in her hair. Her wings folded straight back, like a butterfly's at rest. Every single person in the room had eyes only for her face, her mouth. They were enraptured.

She sang the first note. I understood in my bones what Oscar had said about her voice.

I couldn't have moved from where I stood if I'd tried. I could hardly breathe and I couldn't think. The hairs on my arms stood at attention, and so did my cock. I couldn't help it and I didn't want to.

Simone sang sex.

The first rush of desire. The quickening of a lover's pulse. Lips and teeth and tongues. Taste of salt-slick skin.

I felt it—all of it—as if it were real. As if I were with Amy someplace private. Just the two of us. I could taste her. Feel every curve and angle of her body. My body responded to the heat of hers. Her hands pulling at my shirt. Dragging it over my head. My fingers moving fast on the buttons of her blouse.

The warm, wet plunge of entering.

Amy beneath me, her hair fanned across the pillow. Her legs wrapped around me.

The exquisite tension of sensation, enveloping until there was nothing else. Building and building. Every muscle quivering. No shields. Nowhere to hide.

Amy dug her nails into my back. Called my name.

Only it wasn't Amy's face I saw in that moment. It was Simone's.

Building and building until you came. Hard and long and like death.

I lost myself in her.

I lost myself to time. To space. There was only the feel of the rise and fall of my chest, the fresh warm air in my lungs, the beat of my heart. And Simone's voice.

I opened my eyes, not aware of having closed them. I looked at Simone. She saw me at the same time, her mouth crooking into that same half-grin of Amy's I found so sexy.

Her voice trailed off before the music faded. The drummer played a gorgeous fall of chimes.

I tore my gaze away. I fixed it on shapes across the room in a shadowed corner. A couple of women backed into the wall, entwined so tight I couldn't tell who was who—until one went to her knees. Went down on her partner in the middle of the club. In front of God and everyone.

Someone in the rear of the audience applauded the band. The sound rolled over me like a wave—and broke the magic that had rooted me to the spot.

I pushed my way out of the room on trembling legs. Barely made it to the balcony before they gave out.

I white-knuckled the rickety rail, leaning into it as far as I dared and relieved as hell that I seemed to be alone out there. Just me and a bunch of old coffee cans full of sand and cigarette butts.

The chill seeped in through my clothes and into my joints, and cleared my head until I could think again. I'd never heard—never seen—never felt anything like that before. It was all-encompassing.

The whole world had shrunk until it held only Simone's voice. And I'd felt everything she sang. It felt more than good. It felt indescribable, like a drug. One I could see getting high off every single night for the rest of my life if it didn't kill me first.

Jesus.

A breeze kicked up in cold gusts. I shivered, but couldn't bring myself to put the windbreaker back on—not even when my teeth started to chatter uncontrollably. It was as close as I was going to get to the cold shower I desperately needed. My fingers grew stiff, but I kept hold of the railing. I didn't know how long I stood there.

Scattered crowd noise buffeted me from behind; the show had finally ended.

Marcus the T-shirt Guy joined me on the balcony and raked me up and down with a dash of humor. "First time you've seen them, huh?"

I could only nod.

"Thought you knew what you were getting into since you seemed to know the singer. You'd better sit down, man." Marcus cocked his head at a single plastic chair at the end of the balcony.

I nodded again and peeled my fingers free of the cold metal while Marcus fetched me the seat. Settling into a chair had never felt so good. Or so precarious. I could pass out any minute.

"Busy giving yourself a good case of hypothermia, are you?" Marcus asked.

I found my voice. "I didn't really think about it."

"She makes it hard to think," Marcus said, and lit up a smoke. "You even old enough to be in here?"

I could deny it, but why? "No."

"I don't know how you got past Zeke. He's got a better eye than that."

"The bouncer?"

"Yeah, him," Marcus said. "We're gonna have to sneak you out. Otherwise, you're gonna be in trouble and Zeke'll get fired and beat your ass. Not a good thing."

"Not so much."

Marcus tapped his ashes into the wind. "Just let me know when you're ready to walk and we'll go out the back. Where'd you park?"

"Bike rack."

"I'll need the combination to your lock so I can bring it around."

I'd wanted to trust the guy until he said that. Just trying to be helpful. And maybe larcenous.

My thoughts must've shown on my face, because Marcus raised a brow, managing to keep the good humor and seem offended at the same time.

"I'm staff," he said, "for the singer and the rest of the band. You can find me here every week, if not every night. I screw you over, you can bring your friends and take it up with me later."

I appreciated the honesty. "Sorry. And thanks."

"Forget it," Marcus said. "So, are you capable yet?"

"I think so."

Marcus stuffed what remained of his cigarette into the nearest ash can. "I'm gonna get you out of here, and you're gonna go straight home. Do not pass go and all that. All right?"

I'd come down there to find Simone and talk, not to find her and run away. That was what it would feel like if I took Marcus's advice. But I didn't know if I could handle doing anything else.

"All right, man?" Marcus wanted an answer.

"Yeah. Okay." I'd make up my mind for real after I hit the street.

I took it easy down the back stairs in an unfinished part of the club that still bore a resemblance to the building's original function as a warehouse, complete with a layer of dust six inches thick and empty, wheeled pallets stacked against the walls. I hugged the rail, and the closer I got to the landing, the stronger my legs felt.

One, two, three steps to the ground floor, then ten feet to the back door.

Where Marcus met me, bike in tow. "Zeke asked me no questions; I told him no lies."

"Good for me."

"For both of us," Marcus said. "I don't want my ass beat either." He reached up with a high-five.

I obliged, then watched him disappear into the club again before I even tried my balance on the bike. Shaky going at first, but I caught the rhythm.

Maybe I'd go home after all, seeing as it was almost 2:00 a.m. and it'd take me a while to pedal the five miles to the house, and I had no idea how long it would take for Simone to exit the club and make it back to her bus. Which, I remembered from last night, had up and vanished into thin air some time before 3:30. I could try again tomorrow night.

Nice set of excuses for not taking advantage of already being down here, of having a bead on exactly where Simone was, knowing that my father had short time to live and that Simone was in danger. I was in danger.

I groaned out loud. Who was I kidding?

I was flat-out fascinated by Simone and flat-out terrified of her at the same time. That was why I wanted to head home. I could come back tomorrow with Rude. Strength and safety in numbers, and all that.

Safe. There was that meaningless word again.

Also, it was fucking two in the morning and Rude hadn't called me. I'd had my cell turned off in the club. I turned it on again now.

No missed calls. One text from Amy, who wanted to talk about the party at Zoe's.

If Rude said he'd do something, he did it. The fact that he hadn't churned my gut through a queasy, forward roll.

I sent a text.

Two seconds later, I had incoming—straight out of Rude's mind. *Blood. So much blood.*

And I caught sight of a person-shaped shadow in front of me too late to stop.

I swerved to avoid hitting them and overbalanced the bike. Vaulted the handlebars. Skidded on the heels of my hands across a patch of gravel into the overgrown grass in the ditch on the side of the road and landed with a thud on the hard ground, in serious pain.

The person I'd almost hit came running. I balled up my fist in case this was some kind of ambush. In case I needed to throw a right hook.

Simone leaned over me, meeting my gaze with clear violet-blue eyes.

CHAPTER 18

SIMONE'S VOICE BROUGHT BACK every emotion, every bodily sensation I'd felt in the club. In a split second, she completely destroyed any equilibrium I'd managed to recover.

"Don't talk to me. Please."

"Isn't that what you came here to do?" She bent over me and grabbed hold of my hands.

She pulled me onto my feet. Her touch shook me to my core, and I brushed her hands away. It was damned rude, but she didn't seem to notice, and I hardly cared. I didn't know how to be around her.

"How bad are you hurt?" she asked.

I took inventory: skinned hands, bleeding and slimed with the crushed grass. Jeans, sliced at the knees, which were also scraped up. Helmet-less head, intact and miraculously not concussed. No broken bones, nothing sprained. I'd been very lucky.

Lucky.

I shoved my hand in my pocket. The rock charm? Still there. And in pieces. Damn it.

"Kevin?"

I looked at Simone. She narrowed her eyes and peered *through* me. "We need to get you back to the bus. You're worse off than you look."

"It's nothing that can't be fixed with a whole can of Bactine."

Simone took me by the arm, and this time she wouldn't let me shake loose.

"I'm really sorry about this, Kevin," she said. "I didn't know you'd be back so soon. Or that you'd come looking for me the way you did. You shouldn't have been in there watching me sing."

"It was a lot more than watching."

"It always is," she said matter-of-factly.

It was harder for me to feel embarrassed when she wasn't. "Oscar said the Faery King took you because you can do that with your voice."

"Oscar talks out of his ass a lot, but this time he's right." She wrapped her arm around my waist to support me—awkward—and started walking without waiting for my permission.

"Wait." I glanced over my shoulder. "My bike—"

"Has gone on ahead."

The place where I'd ditched was empty. Just concrete and the shreds of myself I'd left there. "What does that mean?"

She picked up the pace faster than I could keep up. My feet came off the ground. "The fuck?"

"We're going to travel my way, or it'll take forever to get home. Hold on tight."

I had no choice.

We fell just like Rude and I had last night, forever and ever. The street rushed at me. I shut my eyes, unable to break the fall and expecting another bone-crunching jar when we contacted the pavement. It never came.

We sank beneath the earth.

All the breath evacuated my lungs. I tasted road dirt and packed earth and wriggler worms and beetles and rainwater. My lungs began to burn. Pressure built inside—and outside—of me.

I opened my mouth. No sound came out. No air streamed in. I tried to scream. The sound filled my head to bursting.

Just as suddenly as the pressure had grown, it relaxed. I tasted diesel fuel and metal and grime-crusted rubber. And fresh air.

And patchouli and pot and paint and turpentine. We were in the bus.

How—

"Sit," Simone said.

She forced me down onto a vinyl seat, one without a painting but stuffed with blankets. Then she ducked into the back of the bus and rummaged through a lot of paper, judging by the sound. I couldn't see; the light strings in the windows illuminated only so much.

"How, Simone? Did we just go—"

"Underground? Yep."

I leaned back into the blankets.

Simone found what she'd been looking for. Or at least the clatter at the back of the bus ceased. She reappeared, the light dancing on her skin, holding a bottle of something green. "Don't fall asleep here, Kevin."

"Don't worry." That was the last thing I wanted. I ached—every muscle, every molecule. And I didn't want to stay so close to her.

"You'd be surprised how easy it is to drift off," she said. "And you need rest more than anything right now. Healing sleep."

I shook my head. "What I need right now is to find out what's up with Rude. I heard him think."

Simone cocked her head. "He's fine."

"But I heard him."

"Danger's passed," she said. "You'll see."

Relief flooded me. "Great. Then maybe you can tell me how to help my dad—that's why I came here in the first place. Then you can get me home before he wakes up. The charm I had for insurance on that last one is toast because I spilled on the bike, so any help you're willing to give me in that area would be real welcome."

"Ambitious sonofabitch, aren't you?" She handed me the green bottle. "Drink this first."

Now that I could see it better, the bottle was a mason jar, the kind Mom used to use for canning jam this time of year. The liquid inside looked viscous. And vile. "What for?"

"It'll heal you up physically," she said. "That's non-negotiable."

Another bargain. If I gave her what she wanted, she'd give me what I'd come for. "If you poison me, Simone, my ghost will haunt you."

"If I poison you, your body will die and you'll pass from this world without a care. It'd be a relief, not having to carry around the weight you've been hefting these last few months."

Months, not days. She wasn't talking about my new powers or our problems with the Faery King. She was talking about my mom's death. About my dad's drinking.

She sat beside me, leaning forward and resting her elbows on her knees. She didn't bend enough to show me gratuitous cleavage, and that was probably for the best.

"Seriously, Simone. Oscar said my dad came to see you. He said you would know what happened to him. And if my mom…if she actually died or if she was taken."

Her gaze softened. "Your mother's gone, Kevin. She died in the accident, and the Faery King didn't take her spirit."

I swallowed hard. Hearing her say that hurt more than I'd expected —but I'd known the answer before she uttered it. Not because Oscar had said so, but because I'd been there when the cops—real cops—had come to deliver the news.

I'd known when it happened that it was final. It was my dad who'd never accepted it.

"Where did it go?" he asked. "Her spirit, I mean."

"On to wherever it was scheduled to go."

I blinked at her.

"We don't all go to the same place, you know."

"No, I didn't."

Simone sighed. "The important part is that she felt very little pain when she passed over, and that she's golden now, wherever she is."

And all this time I'd thought the important part was she was dead. "So what did you tell my dad?"

"Same thing I just said to you. He didn't buy it. He wanted more proof than my word. He stole something from me."

My father, a thief? "What did he steal?"

"A bottle of potion not unlike the one you haven't bothered to drink yet," she said.

"Fine." I unlatched the lid and sniffed. The stuff smelled like mint. Mint, I could handle. "Down the hatch."

The smell couldn't disguise the flavor—mud that'd been polluted with antifreeze and blended with copper wire. I'd have spat it out, but Simone tipped the bottle so the whole slurry poured into my mouth. I swallowed out of self-preservation and still choked.

Simone pounded me hard on the back and snatched the bottle back before I could throw it at her.

"You really did poison me," I said.

"Medicine always tastes bad, Kevin. You'll be good as new in about twenty minutes. Where were we?" She blew the hair out of her eyes. "Oh, yeah. He took a bottle of Edgewalker Brew, the stuff you use to walk between the human world and the Faery realm. That shit has a very specific time limit. He'd have known that if he'd asked me for it instead of bogarting it. I'd have given it to him, and I'd have told him to be in one place or the other when the juice ran out."

She was saying that it was Dad's own fault he'd ended up broken. He'd blown off the rules and gotten caught. The same thing he'd been giving me hell for.

"He took a potion?" I asked.

"Yes, again. He did."

The memory clicked into place. "Is there an antidote?"

"Sure, Kevin. A tear from the Faery King. He has to give a crap, and he has to grieve. He hasn't done that in a thousand years."

"You're kidding."

"I wish I were." She laid a hand on my arm, like a friend would do. The gesture held no unasked-for energy, no magic, but it melted the defenses I'd managed to put up.

Whether I liked it or not, Simone and I were connected, and the connection was not shallow.

She met my gaze, the corner of her mouth curving. "It's all right, Kevin."

It was anything but. I had a girlfriend—or a girl I wanted to be my girlfriend. I was human and Simone was fae, maybe all the way fae if I couldn't find a way to help her, too. I felt in-lust. I felt protective. I felt confused.

"You want to help me?" she asked.

"You hear thoughts, too?"

She shook her head. "I felt it in you."

Felt. Feelings. Emotions. She could read them. "Stay out of my heart, okay?"

She winced. "You're in over your head, Kevin. Helping me should be the last thing on your mind."

"I'm supposed to let you turn all the way fae? Let you turn into light?"

"It's not up to you. I'm in charge of my own life, and I'll use it how I see fit."

I couldn't argue with that. But it didn't leave me room to help the way I wanted to.

"There's always room for you," she said.

She didn't mean it the way I'd thought it. She meant there was always room for me in her life.

How was I supposed to take that? What was I supposed to say?

I could only circle back around to what we'd been talking about before the conversation had ended up off the rails.

"I have to make the Faery King cry, or else," I said.

"And it can't be because you kicked his ass and his bruises hurt. It has to be emotional."

"Do you know how?"

"Mostly I piss him off. It's not the same." She grinned wryly. "Fighting against my destiny, even unsuccessfully. Associating with humans. The list of annoyances goes on. Luckily he doesn't come here. It's my place. Off limits to His Excellency."

"But my dad—"

"All night, you've talked about your dad. You keep making this whole thing out to be about your father."

"It is."

She opened her mouth to say something, then thought better of it.

"What?"

"There are some things that I can't talk about. Some secrets that I've sworn to keep that way. I'm like a lock without a key. The question is the key."

"What question?"

"The right question."

"How am I supposed to know what the right one is?"

"I can't tell you that."

Infuriating.

"I know you're pissed. I can't do anything about it. There are rules I have to follow."

"Someone tells you what to do."

She nodded.

I didn't need to ask who. It could only be the King. "What is he to you?"

"Besides my liege lord? He's the one who found me in the human world, decided in an instant that I should belong to Faery, and began to turn me. Every day I slide closer to becoming what he is." Her voice began to tremble, and her eyes clouded, as if she were gazing into a darkness only she could see. "Eventually, I'll be one-hundred-percent fae, and it scares the shit out of me."

I didn't say anything. I didn't know *what* to say. How did you comfort someone when you couldn't stop the terrible thing that was happening to them?

She shook her head to clear it, changing gears. "What else did Oscar say today? I know he told you something more—about Tweedledee and Tweedledum?"

It took me a second to catch up. "The cops."

How under orders they'd ruined my life and would keep at it until no one would miss me much after the Faery King took me. Yeah, there was that.

"Oscar does say a lot of things," Simone said. "He's right about this one, too, sorry to report."

"He told me to hide on Halloween."

Simone nodded. "If you can."

"Oscar said the King and the Hunt would take me if I didn't."

"They might have to, Kevin. Any case, you can't stop them if they want to. The King can hear thoughts, and not just when there's life and death at stake. He can read minds. He can read intent. He rules the realm of becoming. He's the most powerful of all of us."

I didn't understand all of that, but I didn't need to for a seed of despair to sprout in my gut.

"No one has ever been able to stop him," she said. "He lets people go when he decides, or if they pass a test, but that's it."

A test? "What do I do now?"

"You'll have to figure that out for yourself, Kevin."

But she was supposed to help me. She was the key, Oscar said.

She rose. "We'll think of something, but right now it's a couple of hours before dawn, and this bus is gonna go poof in a few minutes. I don't want you on it when that happens."

"I get it."

"Your bike's outside. Take it with you, but don't ride it home. It'll take too long, and there's a monster accident gonna happen on your route that you're in danger of joining."

"How do you know that?"

She tapped her forehead. "Where do you think seers like Oscar get their power? From the fae. Faery is the land of ever-becoming, not the land of already-happened. That means we see the things that are about to go down in the human world before they take shape."

"Oh."

She marched me off the bus, double-time. My bike leaned against the side of the vehicle, not a scratch on it. Like I'd never wrecked it.

If I shouldn't ride, how would I get home?

I turned back just as the door hinged shut.

In that instant, the edges of the bus began to fade. I grabbed hold of the bike and hauled it away in the last second before the bus disappeared into Faery, leaving only a tire print in the street dust.

Nothing like standing alone in an alley, abandoned and heart-sore. At least the cuts on my hands had started to knit. The potion had some kick.

I pulled out my phone, fingers twitching. I had no money to pay for a car service. I couldn't call anyone to pick me up without a lot of questions or yelling.

Rude would understand. Rude still hadn't called.

A sweep of headlights at the mouth of the alley blinded me. I raised my arm to shade my eyes, preparing to move. I didn't need to be run over.

With a squeal of brakes, the Explorer stopped in front of me. Rude sat behind the wheel, pale and shaking.

CHAPTER 19

I'D NEVER BEEN so glad to see anyone in my life.

Rude looked like he'd gone ten rounds with a champion heavyweight. He was two shades paler than he ought to be. Dark half-moons bruised the skin beneath eyes. Nose, bloody and possibly broken. A scratch on his right cheek that looked as if a wild animal had clawed him—and not, like, a wild dog. More like a bear.

"Get in," Rude said, his voice hoarse.

I barely managed to throw the bike in the back and get my ass in the shotgun seat before Rude shifted into reverse and backed up at light speed. I caught the armrest with my fingertips, straining to close it—and slammed it just in time to keep the door from shearing off on impact with a utility pole.

Rude didn't even blink.

"You said you were going to stay home, Kev. But you went out. I tried looking for you, but you were just gone. Disappeared. Completely off my radar." Rude fishtailed the Ford onto the street that would take them to the freeway.

"Stop," I said.

He looked at me.

"Now."

He hit the brakes.

I took hold of the wheel. "I've been busted up enough tonight already, Rude. I don't need you taking a turn, too. So the answers are: I changed my mind. It was an accident. What are you talking about, radar? And what the hell is wrong with you?"

Rude glared at my hand on the wheel, but didn't try to move it or say anything about it. He deflated like a punctured tire. "When you carry one of my charms, I have a fix on you."

"You were tracking me? Is that why you gave me the charm?"

"No. Yes."

"Which is it?"

"Both," he said. "You used the charm. I felt it activate. After that, I didn't know what happened to you."

"I didn't know what happened to you, either. You have my phone number. You were supposed to use it."

Rude wiped his forehead with the back of his hand. "It's been a rough night, dude."

"Tell me about it."

Rude launched into a Tale of Weird. He'd showed up at the restaurant like he'd arranged with Oscar only to find it dark with no one there and blood spattered on the back stoop by the dumpster. And there'd been someone in the dumpster. A very unhappy fae that Oscar had beat in a fight. Who took out his anger on Rude.

"How does a fae fight?" I asked.

"Fists. Teeth. Magic," Rude said. "This particular fae, more like soul-sucking."

Soul-sucking? "They can do that?"

Rude nodded. "Some of them."

"And you took this one down."

"Nope. I got him to run away."

"For real?"

"Yeah. It's unbelievable, dude. There I was, ready to drop, easy prey. He takes one more look at me, his eyes go wide, and he bolts. Stepped sideways into Faery with all the usual fireworks—heat, sulfur, flash of light—and then he was gone."

I both did and did not want to know any more than that. The city looked so normal on the surface—shiny people with money and expensive shit, poor people scraping by, poorer people on the streets, and all the other problems that every city in the country had in spades. I'd thought only shady drug deals and shadier business deals happened in the shadows. Now, I knew better.

It was a whole other world out there, and I didn't know how to survive in it.

Yet.

"Will he come back?" I asked.

"Oscar will know."

That guy. "Was this the price he wanted you to pay? Risking getting your soul sucked out?"

"I don't think so," Rude said. "Usually we're talking about helping him reinforce magical protections or some other kind of scut work. Not glamorous. Kinda scary sometimes. But not like this."

I didn't like the direction this was headed. "Why didn't he warn you?"

"You mean, do I think he's cut and bleeding all over the place—or worse?" Rude asked. "Yeah, I do. The blood was his. There wasn't a lot of it, but that doesn't mean much. Like I said, soul-sucking: the weapon of choice."

"How do we find Oscar?" I asked.

"Let me worry about that."

"But—"

"I've tried getting a hold of him nearly every way I know how. No joy. So I did what Oscar told me to do. He said that if anything happened to him, I should find you ASAP."

That didn't seem right. "Why?"

"Because you don't know what you're doing," Rude said. "Yet."

That made me feel strangely better.

"What happened to you?" Rude asked.

"Things got out of hand."

"What else is new?" Rude put the car in drive. Slowly.

I let go of the wheel. "I got the information from our girl on the bus, the answer we were looking for. You're not gonna like it."

I started at the beginning, with our girl away from home and a heavily edited story about how I found her at the club, leaving out the embarrassing parts. I told Rude about the bike accident and the potion. What Simone said about my parents. About the Faery King's tears.

"It's a big break, that info," Rude said. "Even if it's impossible, at least we know which direction to go."

Sunny optimism in the face of the dire. "How do we even start?"

"Not how," Rude said. "When. As in, after we get some sleep."

I laughed. "What is this mysterious thing called *sleep?*"

"That thing you'll get if your dad isn't sitting up, waiting to bust your ass."

"What are the odds?"

"We won't know 'til we get there." Rude mulled that for a minute. "How about I come in with you, in case there's an issue with your father—in case I can smooth it out?"

"Your famous luck, right?"

"Don't leave home without it."

We parked a few houses down and went in the same way I'd had gone out, through the window. Big as he was, Rude fit through the opening. A minor miracle, that.

The lamp was off, but the timer would've taken care of that. I flicked the switch, the halo of light illuminating the bed, where the sheets lay in the exact same crumpled mess as this morning. Dirty laundry spilled over the basket by the closet, yesterday's reeking clothes trailing along the floor. My Chemistry book and notebook, still open to the page where I'd felt frustrated enough to give up.

"What do you think?" Rude whispered.

"It seems okay."

"We should check the rest of the house."

Right. Because we couldn't assume my dad was asleep. He might be out there waiting for me to waltz into the kitchen for a snack in my street clothes.

"I'll go first," Rude said.

For luck.

Even with that, my nerves ratcheted tight. In the clear light of day, I could talk a good game about not wanting to leave my dad alone and really mean it. But in the middle of the night with the whole world asleep and me ignoring every rule my dad set down, the first thing I thought of was the gun in the passenger seat beside him this morning.

I hoped luck would be enough. "Shoes. Sneakers squeak on hardwood."

Rude looked down at his cross-trainers and kicked them off before opening the door to the hall, into pitch black and near silence. A steady stream of voices, punctuated by laugh tracks, bled from under Dad's door at the other end of the hall.

We made a circuit of the house, including the garage and the giant walk-in closet in the den. Finally, only Dad's room remained.

I thought about the gun again and insisted on going in first. If Dad shot an intruder, I didn't want it to be Rude.

Dad lay in bed on his side, curled into the fetal position with the white comforter pulled tight around him, a tuft of his dark hair sticking up from his cowlick. He breathed steady and deep.

The glow of the TV and the commercial depicting the benefits of using the right shampoo turned the foot of the bed into a kaleidoscope of color. On the nightstand, a bedtime glass of water, half-full. Also, Dad's wallet, a handful of folded debit card receipts, and pocket change. No beer cans.

Weird.

Behind all that, the white plastic blinds had been pulled down but not closed, rendering everything Rude and I did visible to anyone standing in the backyard. Not that anyone would be there, watching.

I shuddered and pushed the thought away.

We'd found everything in its place, in a way mostly that made sense. Rude could head home. In a couple of hours, the sun would rise and pretty soon the first bell would ring at school.

I signaled Rude: *Okay to jam.*

But he crept toward the bed and knelt on the side Dad lay nearest to.

No amount of waving caught Rude's attention. I closed in—and nearly pissed myself when my shadow broke the TV's glow and Dad stirred.

I froze. Didn't dare even back up for fear another change in the light would be all it took to wake Dad.

Rude reached out and pressed his palm to Dad's forehead. His lips moved.

The hell?

I couldn't make out the words. But I saw something pass between them—a flash of light so quick that I'd have missed if I'd blinked.

Rude drew his hand away and stood up. He spoke softly, but out loud. "It'll be all right."

I stared at him and then at my dad.

"Time to go, Kev."

Back to my room to gather Rude's shoes and send him on his way. I closed the door behind us and led the way back down the hall.

"What did you do?" I asked.

"Futzed with his memory a little—just enough so he thinks he had a nice meal and the best beer ever, watched the game, and went to sleep. Somewhere in there, he checked on you once and found you asleep in your bed, just like you promised. He felt good about that."

Relief flooded through me.

"That kind of magic is harmless unless you overuse it," Rude said. "He should sleep pretty soundly from here on out, but don't push it. Don't make a lot of noise. In the morning, he'll wake up better than he's been in a long time."

I didn't know what to say—this felt too big for something as plain as "thank you."

"Think you can catch some Zs now?" Rude asked. "There's not much time, but a couple of hours is better than no hours."

I really agreed. "Rude—"

"Don't mention it." He started out the window.

He did not look as relaxed as he should've. He looked as if he was bracing himself for another round of battle.

"You're not going home, are you?" I asked.

He shook his head. "I need to keep looking for Oscar."

"You shouldn't go by yourself."

"You can't come with me, Kevin. Not tonight, any rate. You need to be here when your dad wakes up, no joke."

"What if you run into that soul-sucking thing again?"

"I'll make like Monty Python and run away."

Rude looked like I felt—as if he was running on fumes. "Promise me that if you get jammed up you'll call."

"Sure," Rude said. He seemed like he even half-meant it.

I didn't want to let him go, but short of physically taking Rude down I couldn't keep the guy here. So, I locked the window after Rude went through, and listened for the sound of the Explorer's door, the engine turning over, the telltale fade-out as Rude drove away.

After that, uncomfortable silence.

I dug my Dad's old baseball bat out of the closet. In my Little League days, Dad had my name engraved above the logo. It was the best weapon I had. I hated to think about the implications of using it, but I had to be practical. I stood it up between my bed and the wall and lay down on the bed in my clothes with the light on, the phone on vibrate two inches from my pillow. Just in case.

I tried hard not to think about what might happen to Rude. Or to wonder where Oscar was. For a long, terrible moment, I missed my mom worse than I had in all the time since she'd been gone.

My heart hurt. I pressed the heel of my hand to my chest. It didn't help.

I fell asleep like that and dreamed about Simone and what she'd said. I dreamed Amy was on the bus with us, and that she had some choice things to say to Simone.

I woke with a start to see a familiar shadow in the doorway.

Adrenaline shot through me. I barely dared to breathe.

The shadow dissolved as if it had never been. There was no one there. No strange sounds. No footfalls in the hall. No danger-revealing thoughts that didn't belong to me.

It took a while for my heart and breathing to steady. I didn't think I'd sleep again, but my exhausted body had other ideas. I fought the impending dark with every on-edge nerve until unconsciousness swallowed me whole.

CHAPTER 20

I PADDED BAREFOOT into the kitchen at sunrise to find Dad reading the news on his tablet and finishing up his tea. His fourth or fifth cup, from the number of bags littering the countertop. He wore his work clothes, not neatly pressed but clean, and he'd opened the blinds on the small window above the sink that looked out on the backyard. The morning light gentled the shadows beneath the hackberry tree in the center of the yard, gilding its crown. It was a hopeful sight.

I wanted to feel hopeful.

Dad glanced at me. He looked a little less wild around the edges. Hands? Steady. Eyes? Clear.

"How'd your Chemistry problems go?" he asked.

"Dismal."

"You know, I stunk at Chemistry when I was your age."

"I didn't know." Weird for Dad to volunteer that kind of information. In fact, he'd never talked about his time in school. "Think it's hereditary?"

"Maybe so, Kev. Maybe so," he said. "Funny thing in the news this morning. This place I used to eat at, it went up in flames overnight."

"Which place?"

"Mexican restaurant out west. Damned shame. They had the best enchiladas."

I didn't need him to tell me which restaurant. I didn't need to check the news on my phone to know, either.

I wrapped my fingers around the edge of the counter, hoping Dad didn't notice that I was using it for support—or to keep from punching the wall. Or punching him.

"Did the paper say if anybody got hurt?" I asked.

"Lucky there. It was closed. Everyone had already gone home for the night."

I hoped to God that was true. Because if Rude had gone back there—

"You know what I said yesterday about picking you up from school all week?"

I blinked at him. It took me a second to switch gears from arson—which I felt sure he'd committed—to school logistics. "How could I forget?"

"You were responsible yesterday. Right where you were supposed to be, right on time. You think you could do that on your own today? Can I trust you to do that?"

Why would he have said that? Why would he be willing to let me off the hook so easily? "Sure."

"Good. I expect you to be here when I get home from work. I expect dinner on the table and your homework at least on the way to done, like usual. You don't let me down, I won't let you down. Deal?"

"Yeah. Deal."

He stuck out his hand for me to shake.

I didn't want to touch him. I wanted out of his presence, out of this room, out of the house. I wanted to run until my lungs caught fire and my legs gave out.

I wanted things to go back to the way they'd been before Mom died.

A couple of steps. That was all he expected of me.

I closed the distance between us. He gripped my hand hard enough to rub my knuckles together painfully, but without hostility in his eyes.

I studied his face. No sadistic intent. He was just continuing to crack up, only more quietly than I'd seen earlier.

What Rude did last night had slowed Dad's roll, but the downhill slide continued. What Rude had done was like slapping a Band-Aid over a leak in a dam.

"You going to eat breakfast?" Dad asked.

"I hadn't thought much about it."

The hope I'd felt for a split second while looking out the window had fled, replaced by a sickening cocktail of anger, fear, and heartsickness. The scrapes on my hands and arms stung. I felt as if I'd been beaten, inside and out.

"A bowl of cereal," Dad said. "And some OJ. Start the day off right."

Not what I had in mind, but I didn't want to argue. I got the feeling that, if I pushed, my words might tip the balance in Dad's unraveling mind. I walked on eggshells until Dad left for work.

Only then did I check the news on my phone. The local paper's post about Oscar's restaurant consisted of ten lines. No interview quotes. One photo of a charred building.

That image stayed in my mind as I packed up and walked out the door, worried about Rude. Worried about Oscar. About Dad. About Simone. About myself.

We had the information from Simone, but no way to use it, really. And it was Wednesday already. Hump day. Used to be a day of rejoicing. The week, half over. The weekend, that much closer. I'd never wanted to keep Friday at bay before.

I texted Rude to see if he was okay. He didn't answer.

I tried not to freak out.

The clouds that had been hanging around blew by on a dry north wind. The trees had dropped a load of leaves seemingly overnight, littering the yards and street with mounds of orange, yellow, and brown.

Some of the neighbors had put out decorations, a couple of the porches dressed with freshly carved jack-o'-lanterns and strings of lights that would glow orange after dark. Mr. Morrison, the widower who lived eight houses down, had hung white plastic ghosts and inflatable flying witches from the lowest branches of his live oak.

I stopped cold at the corner where the block split and backpedaled into Morrison's yard. Took cover among the ghosts and witches. I had to squint to see it, and maybe I wouldn't have peeped it at all if I hadn't looked at the south side of the street at that exact moment.

There was an unmarked cop car parallel-parked with the student cars—the same one as I'd seen in my driveway the night of Rude's party. Definitely occupied. By the cops who weren't cops. The Faery King's agents.

After Mom died, even seeing police brought up a kind of PTSD. Took me right back to the middle-of-the-night knock on the door and the way the ground had fallen out from under me and never come back. I started to see things I'd never had to see before—that I wasn't the only one who looked at cops like that. The black and brown kids I went to school with did, too, but not because the cops had brought them bad news—to the cops, those kids were bad news and would never be any other kind.

I'd never thought I'd have to be truly afraid of the police. That they —or some reasonable facsimile—would come after me. They could stuff me in the car and take off with me, and no one would think anything of it. Not only did people around here (read: middle-class white people) generally defer to cops, everyone knew I'd been in trouble with them and thought I *was* trouble.

I could disappear and nobody would bat an eye. Oscar had pointed that out, but I hadn't truly understood it. Until now.

Near as I could tell, the cops hadn't seen me. But they sure did think my name. Loud and clear.

That made my best option sticking close to the house, out of sight. If I cut over a couple of blocks, I could get to school on time.

And what? Go to class like my world hadn't flipped upside down? Hide out? Sure. Because pigs could fly and the Easter Bunny laid chicken eggs. If the Faery King's agents wanted to haul my ass out of there, they'd do it.

I backed up again nice and slow, no big movements to attract attention. One step at a time. Straight into one of them.

Motherfucker.

The cop clamped his hands onto my shoulders, his pinky ring dull in the lack of morning light. I tried to pull away, but the guy was made of muscles. He smelled just like the fallen leaves, musty and papery and cool. He sounded like a normal human asshole.

"School is that way, son," he said. "You don't want to be truant now, do you? On top of everything else?"

"Let me go."

To my surprise, the fake cop did.

I turned carefully. No sudden movements. Caught sight of the fake cop's badge. "What do you want from me, Officer Burns?"

Burns smiled. An undercurrent of magic threaded through his words. "Just keeping an eye on you. Making sure we know where you are and what you're up to at all times. We're gathering evidence on you. And when we've got what we need, we'll take you down, son."

Just threats? No cuffs? No magical whatsits?

Burns wanted me to know that I couldn't hide. I couldn't run. He'd find me no matter what I tried.

I gritted my teeth. "Anything else?"

A breeze kicked up in front of me—exactly in front of me, within a five-foot radius of the cop. He disintegrated from the ground up, flesh and blood and bone drifting apart like leaves. No, not *like* leaves. The man became leaves from bottom to top—a hundred of them, crisp and musty and papery and cool, whirling on the sudden current. Then the air stilled as if someone had turned off a switch, and the leaves floated to earth.

I stared at them for a hot minute, a pile of once-upon-a-Burns, my mind completely blown. I blew out a breath I hadn't realized I'd been holding and drew in fresh air, my body trembling. Another minute to calm the shaking. I allowed myself that much before I turned on my heel and marched down Mr. Morrison's yard to the street.

I walked right past the unmarked car, where Burns's partner sat with the window open, looking at his phone and drinking steaming black coffee from a lidless go-cup.

I didn't give the guy more than a cursory glance. And I didn't look over my shoulder after I passed him. They'd already delivered their threat. Nothing would happen in the next few minutes. Maybe not even today.

Still, I'd never been so glad to step onto school property and duck into the main building. Away from prying eyes.

I skipped the front yard of the school—and Amy—in favor of the smoking area where I hoped to catch Rude. But not only didn't I see him, no ashes graced the spot where he usually hung out and smoked. The worry that sliced through me at breakfast cut deeper.

I pulled out my phone and called. Six rings to voicemail.

On the other side of the skaters' island, a couple of girls sat close. One of them a long-haired brunette and the other a blond with unruly curls down to her shoulders, average cute. I ought to know their names; then again, I did know one of them. Ms. Kinsey from Rude's party and Mr. Nance's office.

I watched her pick a blade of grass and peel it apart, half her attention on her friend and the rest of it on me. Not interested, not inviting, but also not rude.

I walked over.

"Rude's not here," she said. "He didn't show up this morning."

The cereal officially curdled in my belly.

Ms. Kinsey focused on me, staring without blinking.

I should say something to her. Something polite. "Thanks."

"Welcome." She tossed the remains of the blade of grass she'd sheared down and plucked another one. "How are you holding up with everything, Kevin?"

The question startled me. It took me a second to snap to what she meant—the dead girl and the faux cops. And that she'd used my name. "Fine."

"Really?" She cocked her head. "I'd be so freaked out."

She didn't know the half of it.

"Not everyone thinks you're guilty of something," she said. "I just thought you should know."

Not only had I not expected that, but hearing it speared me all the way through. "People taking bets?"

"Your odds aren't all that great."

"Figures."

"Yeah." She grinned ruefully. "I'm Stacy. Short for Anastasia. After the Russian princess."

She seemed amused at her own story. "You egged those lockers from the inside," I said.

"I got a week's worth of detention."

"They obviously don't value that kind of genius around here."

She grinned. "Your girlfriend just came through here. I think she was looking for you."

"Thanks." I started to move on, but Stacy had more to say.

"We should talk sometime."

I raised a brow. "About how to get the best revenge?"

"Magic," she said matter-of-factly.

I stared at her for a minute, waiting for her to laugh or make a face to show she'd been joking, but she seemed one-hundred-percent serious.

Had she heard something? No—she couldn't have. There was plenty of gossip going around about me, but no one could've known that I'd become specially telepathic or that Rude was an apprentice faery seer or that I'd become friends with a girl who had faery wings and lived in a school bus that moved between an alley downtown and the realm of Faery. The truly weird stuff hadn't become public knowledge and probably never would. It was too unbelievable.

But Stacy Kinsey knew something.

"Okay," I said, handing her my polite ticket out of the conversation.

I walked away, but couldn't help glancing over my shoulder on the way into the building. She could be a nightmare. She could be a friend.

She'd helped me, after all, even if it was the kind of help that didn't cost her anything—no, that wasn't true. She'd been seen talking with me, and not with disdain. Right now—and maybe for eternity—people would interpret that as her being on my side. She wasn't stupid. She knew that.

She caught me looking at her and raised her hand in a friendly wave, sealing her fate.

Either being ostracized by association didn't bother her, or she was one of those oppositional people glad to give the middle finger to people who made the rules.

I wished I could be like that.

Catching up with Amy proved hard to do. Every spot I hit—her locker, the snack bar that soaked the air with the scent of French toast and maple syrup—she'd just headed out. I finally found her in class, paging through her textbook.

She glanced up from her book. And texted me immediately.

You didn't answer my text last night.

I'd been so preoccupied, I hadn't remembered. So much had happened, last night felt like a century ago. *I was out. Sorry.*

Forgot your phone?

On cue, Mrs. V walked in. "You know the drill. Phones off," she said in her usual no-nonsense tone, and started to scribble equations on the board before the bell even rang.

Everyone else scrambled to take notes while I tried to think of a witty thing to say to Amy to get myself off the hook. The longer I stared at her text, though, the more I understood that she didn't give a shit about whether I'd forgotten my phone. She wanted to know whether I'd forgotten about her.

Things are hard at home, I wrote, finally. *Can we talk about this after class?*

I'd think what to tell her in the meantime, because I couldn't keep deflecting her questions. Sooner or later she'd start thinking I was bullshit and that she didn't need the trouble.

When class ended, I grabbed my stuff, took her hand, and dragged her out of the room to the nearest quiet place we could duck inside. Which happened to be the library. All the way to the back, as far out of range of the information desk—and prying ears—as possible. The only witnesses? Tall shelves of fiction. The Ks through Ls.

"My dad's not handling things well. That's why I went out. It was a crazy night, and I went over the handlebars of my bike." I held up my scraped hands for inspection.

"Ouch," she said, without empathy. "What are you hiding?"

I blinked at her.

"I'm not stupid. Is it someone else?"

Was I interested in someone else? "No."

For a second, I thought of Simone, who so did not qualify. Except —I squashed the thought that bubbled up from the depths of my mind before I could fully think it. "I'm trying to figure out how to help my dad. He hasn't been okay since—"

Amy's face softened. "Since your mother died. What was her name?"

"Kate." Kathryn Anne Meier Landon. Saying her name hurt. "I didn't think you knew about her."

"It's not a secret, Kevin."

"Yeah, but until lately I haven't been used to too many people paying attention to what happens in my life."

"I like someone, I pay attention," she said.

I leaned against the bookcase behind me. The edge of a shelf poked into my lower back. The musty smell of old paper and binding filled my nose. I couldn't quite look Amy in the eye. "I like you, too."

She closed the distance between us, folded her arms across her chest, and relaxed against the bookshelf beside me. "So your dad's going off the deep end."

"Pretty much."

"Anything I can do to help?"

"I don't know." I only knew I couldn't risk her knowing too much. She'd probably start pretending she'd never met me, and I didn't think I could stand it if she did that.

At the same time, though, would keeping her in the dark put her at risk?

The thought floored me.

This wasn't just about whether her friends would turn on her if she insisted on remaining friends with me, not to mention if we became an actual item. Safety was a consideration. Spending too much time with me could be dangerous. If Burns and his partner moved on me while she was with me, she could get hurt—physically and magically.

If she didn't know anything about what was really happening with me and the fae pressed her for info, she couldn't tell them anything. Would they believe her if she told them she had no idea? Would they threaten to hurt her if I didn't do what they wanted?

Considerations went way beyond whether she liked me or I liked her.

"What's going on in your head?" she asked.

I met her gaze. "I'm worried."

"If you think of something I can do, let me know, Kevin."

"Promise," I said.

She sighed and changed the subject. "You still up for going out Friday?"

"Wouldn't miss it," I said, even though there was every chance in the world I would.

She exhaled a long breath, tension flowing from her shoulders. "You thought at all about the costume party at Zoe's?"

I'd tried not to. It still sounded like torture. But I had a wild thought. A good thought. A way she could help without getting in too deep.

"Do you have a costume in mind?" I asked.

"Not totally. Maybe we could do something couple-ish. Like Morticia and Gomez. Or Sid and Nancy. Or—"

"Or the Faery Queen and King."

She laughed. "Fairies? Isn't that kind of cutesy?"

"Anything but. I'm not talking about tiny garden fairies." I blurted the rest of it before I lost the nerve. "You ever hear of the Wild Hunt?"

"Like the painting in Nance's office," she said.

"Noticed that, too, did you?"

"Hard not to. It's really dark," she said. "I like it. Don't know much about it, though."

"Me neither," I said. "But we can find out. Betcha no one else will have those costumes."

"On that all by itself, I'm sold," she said. "You know the way to my heart, Mr. Landon."

Any other time that would've sent my own heart into my throat, in the best way. Still, it meant a lot. "I've been paying attention."

She touched my hand. "Keep doing that."

"Always."

We came out from behind the stacks to see Mr. Nance settled at a far table. He nodded at us.

Even though the man had been sitting nowhere close, I couldn't help but wonder if he'd heard every word we'd said.

That shouldn't be a big deal. There'd been no secrets, no lies, nothing that should turn his head.

But like Stacy, Mr. Nance seemed to know things he shouldn't. And the question was not only what he knew, but what he might do if he did.

CHAPTER 21

I BREATHED IN the stink of grease so strong, it overpowered the scents of the fish and fries and filmed the air with a sheen of oil that seemed to stick to my hair and skin and clothes. The sympathetic lunch lady at the end of the counter palmed me a handful of extra ketchup packets and smiled at me, good humor in her dark brown eyes.

I scanned the tables, looking for Rude. No joy. My nerves tightened like rubber bands stretched to the limit.

My hackles rose—people stared, some surreptitiously and some openly, with no shame. Every low-pitched voice triggered a certainty that the whole room was talking about me. I knew that wasn't true—logically, it couldn't be—but logic fell bloody and helpless before instinct. It wasn't just the other students who gave me the creepy vibe.

Mrs. V, sitting at a far corner table with her legs crossed, foot swinging like a metronome, watched me like a hawk. My Chem teacher stood in the doorway, gaze focused on me. It was as if they were waiting for me to drop my tray or trip over my own feet. As if they were waiting for me to step out of line.

If I so much as put a toe over the paint, they'd report me, and any chance I might still have at a scholarship would go up in smoke. And they would be happy about it.

I held my breath. I had no reason to think something like that, but if someone asked me to bet my life on it, I would.

I didn't want to be here. I wanted to be out in the world, looking for Rude, but where? The burned-out shell of the restaurant? His house? The empty alley where Simone would appear later?

Where else did he go? Who else did he hang out with? I hardly knew him in the ways that would've been important to me last week. Priorities had changed. The most important thing about Rude was that he had my back when other guys I thought were my friends walked away, and I had his back, too.

There were no empty tables, so I picked one with an empty seat at the end. Before my butt hit the seat, the half-dozen other people at the table stood in unison and flew away like a flock of flushed geese.

Humiliation. Another weight slapped onto my shoulders. It took everything I had not to run for the exit. To sit up taller. To eat my goddamn lunch like I had a right to be there, same as everyone else.

I needed an escape plan. One that didn't threaten my entire future.

In the meantime, what I got was ketchup-drowned fish and chips and a clear line of sight to where Scott sat, laughing it up with his new flavor-of-the-week buddies. The shiner Rude gave him had faded some, from black to purple and yellow.

Amy slid onto the bench beside me, the move sudden and jarring.

"You trying to give me heart failure?" I asked.

She deadpanned. "Do you want heart failure?"

"Considering it seriously."

She followed my gaze to Scott and frowned. "How long have y'all known each other?"

"He moved in next door to us when we were both eight. His parents moved out of the neighborhood just before we started high school."

"I can't believe he did you like that."

"Believe it."

She put a hand on my arm, physically turned me to look at her. "I wouldn't do that to someone. I just want you to know."

I could tell her anything and she would stick. She was for real. I swallowed hard. "I'm like you."

"Fuck the bunch of them," she said, her final word on the subject of Scott. "I went back to the library for study hall. It's amazing what you can find on the Internet about the Faery Queen."

Not exactly what I wanted to talk about right this minute, but information was information and maybe I could turn it to my advantage. "Spill."

"She's capricious. Long black hair. Razor-sharp teeth. Very powerful. And beautiful enough to make men fall in love with her at first sight. There's a story about this guy, Thomas of Er—I can't pronounce where he's from. But he's a real guy from the thirteenth century. The story is called 'The Ballad of Thomas Rhymer'. There's, like, three different versions of the poem, written in old-style English. Right up your alley."

Because I enjoyed reading ye olde English so very much. "Ha ha."

"Anyway, Thomas fell asleep under a hawthorn tree and the Queen was the first thing he saw when he woke. He fell in love and kissed her, and the penalty for doing that was seven years in Faery. He had to go with her. Seven years there was like a hundred years in Scotland."

"When she finally let him go, all the people he knew his whole life had died," Amy said. "Can you imagine that?"

I could imagine. It made me think of Simone, and what would happen to her. It made me think about what Oscar had said, that there was no way to tell how old Simone was anymore because time moved differently for her.

She'd had her life stolen. The King had taken it from her. I could relate.

"Wow," I said.

Amy nodded. "I definitely want to make a costume for her."

Right, because for her this was about the costume party.

"Now we just have to find some information on the Faery King for you."

"I'll be on it tonight," I said.

Amy leaned close and kissed me goodbye, eyes open, gaze locked on mine. In that moment, I wanted more than the taste of her mouth. I wanted to know what it would feel like to hold her hand at the movies, how it would be to learn everything about her. I wanted to memorize everything about her, starting with the feel of her skin against mine.

I watched her head out, following her with my gaze until she disappeared into the crush of people beyond the door. A flicker of movement from Scott's direction caught my attention. Guy was staring at me, the corners of his mouth turned down, eyes sad. He looked almost sorry.

Too bad for him.

The afternoon dragged. Gym turned out to be about volleyball, which I could zombie-walk through—and did. The coach watched me from the corner of his eye the entire hour. After that, I spent my time in study hall figuring out bus schedules to the restaurant and back, and worrying about whether the cops would be parked on the side of the road waiting for me. The librarian stayed within eye- and earshot, inspecting me every ten minutes on the minute.

When the dismissal bell chimed, I made straight for the bus stop behind the school. I got halfway there and stopped on a dime, mouth hanging open. Parked on the street in the same spot as yesterday after lunch? Rude's Explorer.

The car was empty of everything but the big guy's backpack on the passenger seat, a sea of trash from an entire day's fast food chow on the passenger floorboards, and the remains of a super-sized drink in the cup holder. Oh, and Rude's phone. In plain view on the driver's seat.

The light still glowed on the display. Rude had just been there. Had he gone into the school? That seemed likely. I backtracked.

It'd only been fifteen minutes since school let out, so of course the place felt utterly deserted. And it was. Except for Rude, who stood exactly where he'd be on any normal day, wearing his black Hawaiian shirt and smoking with deep, ragged breaths. With Stacy.

She talked at Rude and the big guy listened, never once taking his eyes off her face. Not even when he sensed me walking toward them.

A heartbeat later, Stacy glanced at me. No smile and wave this time.

If the way Rude looked last night had scared me, things plummeted to a whole other level now.

He not only had a set of industrial-sized luggage under his eyes, his face seemed hollowed out there—so much that I could have sworn for a second that I saw his skull. The corners of his mouth trembled as if he was barely holding himself together. And he seemed smaller. Less lucky. Less of a superhero disguised as my friend.

"You're a dead man," I said. "Where you been?"

Rude's voice had grown scratchy since last night. "Close to dead, but not yet. And nowhere good."

"You were supposed to let me know what happened. Whether you found Oscar."

"I promised if I got jammed up I'd call," Rude said. "I'm fine."

"Have you looked in the mirror?"

"That bad, huh?" Rude took a shaky drag on his smoke, pitched it, and smashed it out with the heel of his shoe.

"What went down, man? I saw the article in the paper this morning."

Rude fumbled in his pocket for his portable ashtray tin. "I found Oscar on the singer's bus."

That didn't make any sense. "But the bus disappeared last night into Faery. I saw it go."

"Exactly."

"So, what? You went to Faery to find Oscar?"

"Yeah."

I stared at him. I stared at Stacy. She'd listened to all of this without batting a lash. As if we were talking about grocery shopping or taking out the trash.

She held up a hand to halt the conversation. "I told Kevin we should talk, but maybe this isn't the time."

Rude shrugged.

"I'm out for now. See you both later." She turned to walk away, and I'd have stared after her if Rude hadn't opened his mouth again, drawing my attention as solidly as if he'd put a hand on my cheek and physically turned my face toward his.

"I had a little trouble bringing back Oscar from Faery."

A little trouble. *A little trouble* had turned him into a shadow of himself overnight.

"What—like monsters?" I asked.

Rude shook his head. He tried to open the tin, but his fingers didn't do the job. I took the thing from him and pried the lid open, getting a noseful of burnt tobacco and paper.

Rude started to say one thing, but changed his mind. "It's a scary place, dude. I'll tell you later."

In other words, not here. "How's Oscar?"

"He'll live." The look in Rude's eyes testified that it'd been a close call.

"Where's he at?"

"My house."

"With your parents?"

"In the pool house, Kev. Laying low. He's still in danger. If the enemy finds him there, it's gonna get very ugly. It's not safe. Nowhere is."

"And you left him to come here because why?"

Rude sighed. "That girl I was talking to?"

"Stacy."

"Yeah, her. She had some important information to give me about how to counter the magic that almost took me down today."

"She'd know that how?"

"She's a witch."

I blinked at him. "A what?"

"Never mind, Kev. Let's go."

"Back to your house." Of course that was where we'd go.

"For as long as you can stay."

Right. I had my dad to think about. And if I didn't, Rude would do it for me.

The big guy bent to pick up the butt from the ground. It took him two tries to get down there without toppling.

"Keys, man." Rude had no business driving.

On the way to the Explorer, I told him about the unmarked car and Officer Burns, and I drove a circular route to Rude's house.

All the lights were off in the front room of the pool house when we got there, and Rude didn't flip the switch when we went in. We followed the pathway through the wicker furniture maze by the late afternoon light that streamed in through the window blinds and by the glow that issued from the crack beneath the closed bedroom door in the back. The air tasted of chlorine and copper—blood. A lot of blood.

Oscar slept like the dead on one of two made-up twin beds. The rise of his chest was so slight, at first blush he didn't appear to breathe at all. In the light of the ceiling fan's lamp, almost all of the brown looked to have been bleached from his skin, rendering it not just pale, but nearly translucent, the curved stripes of the capillaries beneath the surface prominent.

On top of that, someone had worked over his face the same way they'd done a number on Rude's. A nasty gash started at the top of Oscar's shoulder and vanished under the once-white fabric of his tank. His jeans had been shredded below the knee, the skin there a mesh of scabbed scratches. His bare feet looked to be the only part of him untouched. Battered steel-toed work boots stuffed with balled-up socks lay at the foot of the bed.

"Christ," I whispered.

"Yeah," Rude said.

"He was like this when you found him?"

"He was awake. He's the one who got us out of Faery and back home. If it hadn't been for him, it could've been a lot worse."

In other words, Rude had been lucky again. It scared the shit out of me to think what *unlucky* might've looked like. "You want to tell me about it now?"

Rude settled on the empty bed, box spring creaking under his weight. "Stacy helped me track Oscar last night. We followed the energy trail he took to get away from the soul-sucker. It went straight into Faery."

"She's the one who told me you weren't at school this morning."

Rude nodded. "I told her you might come looking for me."

"You told *her*."

"Look, dude, we each have the stuff we have to do. I needed to go after Oscar. You needed to be in school."

He was right. I accepted that. And I felt like an asshole. "School shouldn't seem important when people's lives are on the line."

"What did you do at school today, Kev?"

In spite of all the teachers' eyes on me, I hadn't gotten popped for any real or imagined infraction. I'd discovered that Amy didn't scare easily. And one other thing had happened.

"I got some information on the Faery Queen that we might be able to use."

"That's important," Rude said.

I nodded.

"When everything is said and done, your life's not gonna be over," he said. "You'll still have to live it."

I looked at Rude as if he was an alien. "You really think everything will go back to normal?"

He sighed. "There will be a new normal."

"Unless the Faery King takes me."

"I'm not planning on that. Are you?"

"How can you be this calm?"

"Would it help if I lost it?"

I laced my fingers and rested my hands on the crown of my head. If I pressed down hard enough, maybe it would keep my head from exploding. "Halloween is almost here, man. We have no idea how to get on top of this."

"This isn't like a test you can study for, Kev."

"Are you giving me shit about studying? About being smart? Because you're, like, the class clown and I'm some kind of joke?"

He shook his head. "Dude."

"Dude, what?"

"Don't try to pick a fight with me. It's not going to work."

"Why not?"

"Because I won't let it. We need to be together on this or it's gonna be a lot worse."

"Than what?"

"Than anything you can imagine," he said. "That's not a dig. That's the honest truth. Can you chill?"

I didn't even know what that meant anymore, and I couldn't handle another ounce of weight on my shoulders. One more thing would be the final straw. It would break me.

If that happened, I could kiss my ass goodbye, along with Dad's and Rude's and Simone's. Anyone else who got in the way—like Stacy and Amy—too. The only way out of this hopeless mess was through it, and to get through it I had to get it together.

"Since when did you become my big brother?" I asked.

"Since Oscar went down, and now I have to do his job. He wanted you protected."

"I didn't ask you to protect me," I said. "Either of you."

"You need it, dumbass."

I opened my mouth to reply, but Rude bowled right over me. "You're only starting to get an idea of what you're dealing with. I'm trying to help you, dude, but I don't know a quarter of what Oscar does. I don't know what I'm doing. I'm flying on instinct and my stupid fucking luck. I'm as in over my head as you are."

"Who's picking a fight now?"

"I'm not," he said.

No, he wasn't. He was telling me that he was afraid that he would screw everything up, and he was carrying everyone's fate on his shoulders. If he wasn't standing on the edge of a cliff, losing his balance, he was approaching it. He needed me to know. He needed me to understand.

The least I could do was try. "Okay."

Rude shook his head. "It's not okay."

"What are we gonna do about it?"

Some of the mad drained out of Rude, and the mattress sagged under his weight. "You wanted to know what happened to us in Faery. Near as I can tell from Oscar, he took refuge with the singer. It took everything he had to get there, to her bus, because he had to go into Faery to do it. She said she only let him on because of how bad he was hurt. And because of you."

I let my hands fall to my sides, where they curled into fists of their own accord. I looked at them, then at Rude again.

"Yeah, I know, dude. I told you already she likes you."

"Likes?" I asked. "Or *likes?*"

"Dumbass," Rude said again, only this time it sounded like a term of endearment.

There was that straw I couldn't handle—that I didn't want to handle—floating down to land on top of me. I waited to see if I would crumble. When it didn't happen, I exhaled a shaky breath and changed the subject. "So what was it like, Faery?"

"You know how I said before that it was scary?" Rude rubbed the bridge of his nose. "Everything you've ever been afraid of, everything you're afraid you might find there or that might happen to you there —it meets you, gets in your face. Real ghosts from the past. Real monsters, Kev. The soul-sucker? He was there. Ten feet tall and bullet-proof. Much worse than he was when I ran into him at the restaurant."

I shuddered.

"No kidding," Rude said. "You'd better be thinking about what you'll run into and how you're gonna handle it."

To free my dad from the illusion stealing his mind, I would have to coax a tear out of the Faery King. Chances were, I'd be doing that in Faery. I'd have to run the same terrible gauntlet.

I'd have to face my own nightmares and survive.

"What's next?" Rude asked.

I couldn't believe he was asking *me.* But he was right—if we were going to get through this whole and alive, we'd have to do that together. Rude offered me the chance to do more than react to whatever came flying at me. He was asking me to think. To anticipate.

If he knew less than Oscar, and I knew less than him, and if

Simone wasn't available and panic was out of the question, then I had to throw the idea that knowledge would set us free out the window. I thought about the way I'd felt at lunch, with all eyes on me in the cafeteria. I'd thought about what I knew to be true versus what my gut insisted was true. Logic versus feeling. Higher learning versus the intuition that people called survival instinct. I needed to learn to listen to that, because in this fight, I had little else.

If I couldn't figure out the enemy's next move, I could force the enemy to react to mine.

CHAPTER 22

I TOOK A SHORTCUT home on my bike and let myself in the back door, partly in case of the cops and partly in case Dad pulled in earlier than expected. The house was empty and lonely, the ghosts of this morning's breakfast and conversation hanging in the air. I had an hour to put my plan in motion. Best get it done.

I opened the fridge. The contents told a sad story: no meat tonight. There was none to speak of in the pantry, either, except a couple of cans of tuna fish, and the plan demanded better than tuna casserole. I needed to throw out some stops.

I boiled pasta and threw some olive oil, onions, and garlic in a saucepan—the beginnings of a bangin' sauce. I tossed a salad and saved some time with pre-packaged garlic bread from the grocery store. Into the oven it went.

The spicy and savory scents wafted through the front of the house, sure to satisfy Dad that I'd followed orders. A good thing, too, since his key turned in the front door lock just as I drained the pasta.

Dad hung his keys on the brass holder in the entryway and set his briefcase on the floor against the wall. "We having that Italian thing?"

"That's the one," I said.

He loosened his tie and washed his hands in the kitchen sink. "Feed the bear, son."

"Hungry, are you?"

"It was a long day." He dried his hands on a dish towel and fell as much as sat in his chair at the head of the table.

I served the pasta and squirmed through the awkward grace Dad offered. After that, neither of us said much for the fifteen minutes it took to wolf down most of dinner.

"Today at work the manager announced the firm is merging with a bigger fish."

That didn't sound easy. "What does that mean for you?"

"Probably nothing. My department might be consolidated with the one at the big firm. If they already have someone doing that job who they like better, or who they can get to work for less money than I make, I might need to start looking for another job."

Scary—scarier than the Faery King. "When will you know?"

"In the next month or so," Dad said. "I don't want you to worry about it. I don't know why I even told you."

Because he couldn't handle keeping it to himself, that was why. He didn't have any friends left that I knew of; he'd let them all drift away—or in some cases, sent them away—after last Halloween. He neither needed nor wanted company to help him drown his sorrows.

But me? I got to take on problems I had no way to solve. I got to be the repository for his worries. He left them with me so he could feel better.

I got up from the table and started to scrape plates and load the dishwasher. It was something to do while I tried with all of my willpower not to let fear of having less—or no—money steamroll me. I needed to focus. Eyes on the prize.

"How was your day?" Dad asked.

"Fine."

"Fine, he lied." My dad flashed a wry grin that I wanted to wipe off his face.

"I'm having a hard time in some of my classes. People are still treating me like a super-freak and I'm still grounded. What else do you want to know?"

"What's for homework?"

English? Chem? Stat? I could answer with any of those and the night would probably go the same way the last few had gone. I could hand Dad a beer or three and wait until he wandered back into his room, then hack his password and check out his search history and bookmarks, looking for his research on the Wild Hunt.

I'd spent so much time worried about Dad, walking on eggshells, wondering whether something I said or did would be his final straw, wondering whether he'd crack up sooner rather than later. The whole time I'd pretended to be doing as I was told or trying not to get caught doing what I wanted—needed—to do, he'd pretended to the best of his ability that everything was normal.

There was that word again. I hated it. There was no such thing.

He'd come to me for help with everything else. Dealing with Mom's death. Financial worries. He hadn't come to me about magic or the fae or revenge or the possibility of bringing Mom back. Why not? Because I'd call him crazy?

I knew he wasn't—not about most of it.

I didn't know whether the Faery King and his minions counted on us continuing to pretend, and I didn't have a lot of strike-back options. Not yet.

Lobbing a bomb into the mix might be the stupidest thing I'd ever done. Or it could be the smartest. Either way, it was a wild card. None of us knew what would happen.

Time to find out.

I leaned against the counter and wiped my damp hands on my jeans. "What do you know about the Wild Hunt?"

Dad blinked at me. "What?"

"The fae that ride horses in the sky on Halloween night, kidnapping humans."

He froze for a split second, then recovered. "You saw that image on my computer the other night."

I nodded.

"That's why you're asking."

I shook my head. "I'm asking because the world's going to hell all around us. I can hear people's thoughts when they're in danger—it's my new thing. Those cops that came by the house looking for me aren't actual cops. They're not human, anyway. And you're an arsonist —don't try to tell me it wasn't you who burned down Oscar's restaurant. I don't want to hear it."

He stared at me.

"I saw you in the parking lot across the street, Dad, when you went there to case the place. You had a gun. Where's the gun now?"

He narrowed his eyes. "I don't remember that."

Maybe he didn't. Maybe he did, but didn't want to admit how far gone down the fae rabbit hole he'd fallen. "Gun," I said.

"I tossed it in the bayou."

Convenient. And unlikely. A gun was worth money, which we needed more of. If he'd gotten rid of it, he'd have pawned it—that was the logical part of my brain talking. Did he have any logic left?

"Is it in the nightstand drawer in you room?" I asked.

He didn't say yes. He didn't say no.

"I need you to lay off the Faery King," I said. "Mom is dead. He doesn't have her."

He set his elbows on the table and cradled his head in his hands. "Who told you all of this?"

"Oscar," I said. "My friend Rude, his apprentice. And the singer."

Dad met my gaze. "They're lying."

I could see how he wanted to believe that. "I'd give anything to have Mom back, too."

"You don't understand," he said. "She was your mother, but she was my wife."

No one had ever said anything like that to me. As if I loved her less. As if I needed her less. As if my pain couldn't compare. "Are you fucking kidding me?"

"You're cussing at me? At *me?*" He planted his palms on the table and pushed to his feet.

I shoved away from the counter and planted my feet, solid and strong. He was going to yell. He had no right.

He started to spin up, every syllable louder than the last. "Disrespectful—"

I wanted to match the volume. I forced myself to stay calm. I forced my voice to remain low. "No."

He took a step toward me.

"Stay over there, Dad."

"You—"

"This isn't about me," I said. "This is about you. You're losing your shit, and you need to stop. Get it together. You're supposed to be the adult here. You're supposed to know what to do, and instead you're screwing it all up."

He glanced down, studying his shoes, his ears and cheeks flushing red.

My heart stuttered in my chest. I'd gone too far in my truth-telling. He was pissed. He'd ball his hands into fists and things would get out of hand. I'd have to leave. I'd have to run or get hit—or hit back.

But then he looked at me again, the anger draining out of him, eyes suspiciously wet. He wasn't pissed anymore. He was ashamed. I'd shamed my own father.

I didn't know what to do or say to undo that. To fix it.

His voice shook. "Go to your room. Go to bed. I don't want to see your face until the sun comes up again. You got that, Kevin?"

I turned on my heel and walked away. I kept it together until I'd shut my bedroom door and locked it.

Pressure started to build in my chest until it felt bigger than my whole body. It bulged inside my skin. It roared in my blood. It felt strong enough to break bones. To break me. I needed to get it out. I didn't know how.

I lay down on my bed in my clothes and sneakers and curled into a ball, doing everything I could to contain the urge to scream, because if I started I didn't know whether I'd be able to stop.

I listened, holding my breath until I had no choice but to exhale. A half hour later, Dad's footfalls in the hall and the gentle snick of his bedroom door signaled that he'd had enough for the night. The low buzz of his TV infiltrated my room.

Should I stay here? Should I go? Would he work himself into a rage and beat down my door? Would he bring the gun with him?

Or would he drink himself to sleep?

The soft mattress seduced my bones. I so badly needed to shut down—to rest my body, to let go of the pressure and the worry that held me awake and alert. Against my will, I closed my eyes, thinking about Rude's story of monsters that started out as fears and ended up solid and real in the realm of Faery.

Sleep stole me down.

I snapped awake at 2:34 a.m. by the glowing red display of the clock on my desk. The ceiling fan whirred. The house creaked and settled. Outside, the wind rattled dead leaves on their branches.

My breath came fast and hard—no idea why. I didn't remember having a nightmare, but every muscle in my body tensed. Every cell balanced on edge. Instinctively, I reached for the baseball bat at my bedside and wrapped my fingers around the handle and waited, as still as possible.

Time stretched. The minutes passed. With. Perfect. Agony.

But nothing happened. Gradually, my breathing settled. I relaxed my legs. Wiggled my fingers. Loosened my grip on the bat as adrenaline seeped away. I drifted again, exhaustion taking over. Dreams reached up to drag me under.

I felt grass beneath me, manicured to obsessive perfection—I sat on a lawn, the lush scent of roses on the autumn wind that lifted my hair from my forehead and cooled my skin. The branches of the great live oak to my right rustled, the shadows of its leaves dappling the afternoon sun.

I caught sight of a black bird and watched it pick at the ground with its beak. It tilted its head at me. Maybe it looked at me the way another human person would. Its eyes seemed too wise for a bird's.

It made me nervous, but I didn't want to turn away. The only other thing to see around here happened to be Mom's grave, and I didn't want to acknowledge that the grass I perched on had grown thick and rich over the hole where the cemetery workers had buried her. But the crow flew off and left me alone with that undeniable fact.

Mom was dead, but Mom was also right here, solid and real as life.

She settled across from me, looking just the way she had the last time I'd seen her, the night she'd left to go meet her girlfriends at the movies.

She'd ruffled my hair back then, which I hated because for crying out loud I wasn't a little boy anymore. And she wore the silver filigree earrings I'd given her for her birthday.

"You don't have a lot of time, Kevin, so pay attention."

"It's a couple of hours before the alarm goes off."

"Oh, you know better than that."

I supposed I did, but I was afraid to ask myself why. "How come you're here?"

"Because you wouldn't listen to your gut. You're not safe. Can't you hear him?"

"Who?"

"Your father. Thinking about those craptastic cop wannabes in his sleep."

I didn't want to think about that, and the danger it might mean. Not with her sitting close enough to touch. "Don't worry. I can handle it."

She shook her head. "Kevin Xavier Landon, you listen to me. You wake up now or you won't hear them in time."

CHAPTER 23

I BOLTED UPRIGHT, bile in my throat. My room was dark and no light leaked through the cracks in the blinds—the night still held sway. I was alone in my room, thank God. But I wasn't the only one awake in the house.

Ordinary noises issued from the general vicinity of the kitchen. The fridge opened. The plastic top of the milk container popped. The burner switch on the gas stove click-click-clicked and *whoomfed* to flame. All normal sounds. Except the cadence of them felt wrong.

Dad didn't walk or lift and place the teakettle on the stove with that rhythm. And he sure didn't hum while he cooked.

Either I'd driven Dad over the edge last night and everything about him had changed, or someone completely else was making a middle-of-the-night snack.

I grabbed hold of the bat again and snicked open my door. I peered out. Dad's door? Closed. The murmur of the TV leaked through the gaps between the door and the frame. Nothing out of the ordinary there.

Soft light poured from the front of the house, illuminated a circle of hardwood at the hall door. The humming in the kitchen had risen to song now. The timbre of the voice struck a chord of longing in me.

Not the kind of longing where you daydream about things (a vacation from your life a pocket full of money a brand new drop-top with a banging sound system so you didn't have to walk every-damned-where) or people (Amy) (Simone) and imagine you can reach out and touch them. This desire started in the soles of my feet and worked its way through my veins, pumping so fast and hot, my heart almost couldn't handle it. The kind of wanting that could make me fall in love at first sight—or brutally kill. The kind that could make me give up my life.

It grabbed me by the throat and dragged me into the kitchen, the ball bat brushing the floor behind me. My fingers wanted to let go of it. I held onto a shred of will for dear life.

The man standing in front of the counter—and it was a man, near as I could tell—hadn't turned on any of the lights, unless you counted the burner on the stove. He glowed. Light flowed from his skin like a waterfall, dripping onto the floor and filtering through the air in a bright mist. Not like sunlight—like moonlight, starlight.

That glow reminded me of a weekend camping trip with Mom and Dad. I couldn't have been more than twelve. The full moon shone bright in the sky, and so far out of the city without interference from the streetlights and halogens and giant, come-hither spotlights, you could see an entire sea of stars overhead. The whole Milky Way.

The Milky Way Man standing in my kitchen wore a brown leather vest and pants. Not biker leather or rocker leather. This stuff seemed soft and way more expensive than anything I'd seen on a trip to the mall. The man's shirt wasn't just white. It looked like fresh cream. And his feet? I couldn't get a fix on them. One moment, boots. Another, paws. Gray and black, like a wolf's.

The guy twirled a soup spoon from the silverware drawer in one hand. He'd assembled a mug with a handful of bags from the Super Secret Dad Tea Stash, where no one else dared to tread. Who didn't love a cuppa in the wee hours of the morning?

His voice sounded like leaves shimmering in the wind. "There's enough for two if you'd care to join me."

I cleared my throat. I intended to say something menacing, but literally couldn't. My words refused to obey, and something dumb came out instead. "Actually, there's just enough for my dad's breakfast the next couple of days."

The man turned around and showed his face. Golden-brown hair fell to just past his shoulders. His lips curved in a smile that sent a chill to my marrow, with the same too-sharp teeth Simone showed when she grinned. He had an aristocratic nose. And those eyes, violet rimmed with gold, pinned me to the spot. They could see every thought in my head, every feeling in my heart, every spark in every nerve cell as it fired. There would be no holding back under that gaze.

He was different—much more powerful—than Simone. Or "Officer" Burns or his partner. None of them could do this to me—that I knew of. And Simone had said only the Faery King could read minds.

My knees buckled. Not from shock, but because my first instinct was to kneel. I fought it. "You're the King."

The Milky Way Man nodded. "I thought it was time we met."

"The hell do you want from me?"

The King's smile turned cold.

The grin turned me to ice. My body started to fold in on itself for warmth. Any second, my teeth would start to chatter. "Do you mind?"

The King laughed. In an instant, the chill abated. The kettle began to whistle. He whisked it off the heat and poured without spilling a drop. Turning off the burner? An afterthought.

The Faery King, in my kitchen. Making a cup of tea.

"I wanted to see you, Kevin Landon. I wanted to see *into* you. And, now that I have, I'm certain as to what must be done."

"What must be—what are you talking about?"

"You have no idea how rare your gift is."

"I never wanted it."

"Would you give it up if you could?"

The answer came out in a rush. "Yes."

"I'm here to help you do that."

I stared at him. "How?"

He set the cup of tea on the table. "Drink."

It looked like a normal cup of tea. No weird colors. No strange smells. "What's in it?"

"A removal spell."

"To take away my ability to hear thoughts."

He nodded.

The relief that flooded through me made me want to swoon—until a nagging thought speared my mind like an ice pick. "Will it fix the problems I have at school?"

People talking behind my back. Teachers treating me like I'm one step away from criminal.

"It contains a component of forgetting. You won't remember me or any other fae or fae-connected person you've met. The world will forget your troubles. It will be as if you'd never gone to the party the night this all began."

That was almost everything I could possibly want in the world. If I could just go back to the ways things were last week, keep my head down, do what it took to get that scholarship and get out—what wouldn't I give for that?

"What about the singer?"

"She's not your concern."

"She's my friend."

"She's no one's friend. She's beyond your help. Let it go, Kevin."

I shook my head. "What about my dad?"

"What about him?"

"You need to let him go, too. Let him drink the forgetting tea."

"He has."

"It didn't work?"

"He didn't want it to work."

Why wouldn't he have wanted that? If the tea could've helped him forget about Mom's death, if it could've eased his grief, it would've been a blessing. He would've been able to go on. To live without torturing himself twenty-four seven.

He could've been my dad in all the ways that mattered to me.

"Why?" I whispered, my voice strangled with feeling.

"He didn't want to lose the memory of his wife. He didn't want to lose the memory of his son."

My heart stuttered inside my rib cage. Understanding flooded me suddenly and painfully, as if I'd crashed through the crust over a frozen lake, plunged feet-first into deep water. The price for forgetting—for saving himself—had been too high.

"You'll do what I ask," the King said.

"Or you'll kill me?"

"I'll kill your father."

I started toward him, hand tightening into a fist.

"Don't, Kevin." He said it softly, the way you'd talk to a small child who doesn't know any better. "I'll leave the tea for you. You decide where to go from here."

He closed the distance between us. As he drew nearer, I saw that he had no flesh and blood. His body only looked solid, but it was made entirely of light.

I understood then in a way that I hadn't yet been able to before that he wasn't human. He'd never been human. He had no human parts, no human feelings. He was as alien to me as a creature from a science fiction movie and I didn't know anything about him or his people. His *species*.

He stepped sideways and vanished, leaving me alone in the suddenly dark kitchen as the clock struck four. The silence that descended felt as deep as the ice water I was drowning in. All encompassing.

It was too quiet. As if I were the only one left in the house. The only sounds I heard were my own shaky breathing, the rush of blood inside my head, the ticking of the clock.

I could no longer hear the murmur of the TV in Dad's room.

CHAPTER 24

THE IMPRINT DAD'S body had left in the sheets as he slept? Still warm and rumpled, scented with his soap and the gel he wore in his hair. On the nightstand, his spare change, wallet, and keys. The plastic blinds covering the open window behind the bed clattered as the wind gusted.

I reached up and pulled the window closed. The squeal of the glass in the frame sliced through me.

Dad was gone.

The King had taken him somehow. Maybe by magic. Maybe the faery cops had done it while the King distracted me.

One plan of action after another swept through my mind. Go see Simone? Too late. Oscar? Laid out unconscious in the pool house. Rude? Taking care of Oscar, keeping him safe. Who else was there? Only me.

Fixing this was up to me.

I screamed out loud. Loud enough to alarm the neighbors. To shred my throat.

It didn't help.

I made my way back to the kitchen, where the tea sat on the table, exactly where the King had left it. Waiting for me to decide. Waiting for me to sip. To forget. To become the someone else I'd always wanted to be. A new person filled with possibilities. Someone you could like when you first met them because you didn't already know anything prejudicial. Someone who could be whatever he wanted and not a kid without a mom whose dad drank and tried to kill people.

Becoming that someone meant abandoning my dad. Abandoning Simone. Forgetting them and the terrible trouble they were in, forgetting Rude and Stacy and God only knew who else. Maybe I had what it took to help them, or maybe Simone was right that I didn't stand a chance. I was new to my powers, and the situation demanded that I know what the fuck I was doing.

The price of saving myself was the destruction of people I loved and people I barely knew—human beings with lives and loves and light inside them. Maybe it wouldn't be my fault if they died or lost everything, if the King's plans for them became reality. If I couldn't do anything to stop that.

But if I could? If I could help and refused? I couldn't do that. I wasn't built that way. It was more than that, though.

Even if I couldn't stop the worst from happening, I could do *something* for my people. All of them, from Dad to Stacy, Simone to Oscar, Rude to Amy. I had to try. I had to give my all, even if the depth of the water overwhelmed me, even if the current carried me faster than I could handle, even if I crashed on the rocks and broke.

I'd thought I understood what that meant before. What I could and would do when it mattered most. I'd never had a clue before.

The click of a key turning in the front door lock raised all of my alarms. I couldn't make my legs move fast enough, as if I could only mobilize in slow motion, running for the entry, clumsy and off-balance, tripping over the thick rug behind the door as the knob twisted, catching my balance by spilling into the wall.

Only Dad and I had keys. No friends. No neighbors. It had to be Dad.

But that made no sense. The King had him. Had he escaped?

Rude pushed open the door with surprising stealth for a big guy in a bright pink Hawaiian shirt. I met his gaze, read a question in his eyes that my expression seemed to answer.

The corners of his mouth turned down. "What happened?"

The day was half-gone. How had I not noticed the light coming in through the windows? The King must've done something. Brought the strange flow of fae time with him into our world. Spelled me somehow. Or, like Dad, I'd lost my shit without realizing, and it'd taken hours for my equilibrium to return.

I pushed away from the wall on wobbly legs. Rude grabbed my shoulders, holding on until I steadied. The sensation of being moved bodily by another human being jarred me to different level of consciousness. I felt awake. More awake than I'd ever been in my whole life.

"Dude. I looked for you at school. You weren't there. I got called to Nance's office—he's the one who told me you were in trouble. He wrote me an excuse to take to the office. Like, a family emergency note. He said to go get you."

"Mr. Nance, the school counselor."

"I know, right?"

I rubbed my mouth.

"You look like you're in shock, dude. What happened?"

I told him the story. Halfway through, I had to sit down. Rude let me slide to the floor and settled down across from me. He was quiet for a while after I finished, mulling what I'd said.

"How did Mr. Nance know to send you?" I asked.

"No idea."

"He's like the cops, man. Not really a counselor."

"No, he's a counselor. He's just, I don't know, connected."

"To what?"

"Not my story to tell."

"For real?"

"You can ask him if you want. Or ask the singer."

"The singer?"

"Like I said. What are we gonna do?"

Not me. We. "Things are gonna get hard from here."

"They weren't hard already?"

I rolled my eyes. "You know what I'm saying. I'm talking about going against the King. About doing the seemingly impossible."

"If you're in, I'm in, Kevin."

I studied him. He wasn't bluffing. He wasn't the kind to look for a better offer somewhere else. If he said he was down, he was down. And, better than most, he understood the risk.

"I have to pretend I drank the tea and do my day like everything's normal. If you think that would work. I mean, will the King just know somehow?"

"I don't think so."

"We'll go with that, then."

"What are you thinking about doing?"

"Buying time until I figure out a next step."

"I don't have any better ideas."

"I'll have to act like I don't know you."

"You wouldn't be the first, dude."

I cracked a wry grin. A heartbeat later, a wave of grief crashed over me and erased the smile. I stood carefully, testing out my legs. When they didn't give, I went to my room and packed what I could shove into my backpack, filling in all the empty spaces. Enough clothes for a couple of days, in case I needed them.

If I couldn't find a way to free us all from the King—

I couldn't think like that. No compromise. No surrender.

I threw on some clean clothes and shrugged into my jacket, combed my fingers through my hair. Last minute, I remembered to grab my toothbrush, and met Rude by the front door.

He looked me over. "Live to fight another day, dude."

"Agreed."

He left on his own first, storming off as if he were hurt and pissed. An Oscar-worthy performance, for whatever it was worth—a lot, I hoped. I watched him stalk down the street, kicking up piles of fallen leaves, hands fisted in his front pockets, and shut the door, counting the minutes until I could follow.

Silence settled around me again, this time, even louder than before. It was a warning—that ancient forces more powerful than I was could gut my life in the space of a moment. I'd lost so much already, but I still had so much to lose. It was also a reminder that magic was real and a part of me. I needed to stop fearing it and start using it. It was the only way through this nightmare.

When I stepped out into the world and locked the door behind me, the realization hit me hard: if I failed, I might never come home again. I turned on my heel and walked away, trying not to glance over my shoulder. I had to move forward. Focus.

The wind gusted, rustling the branches on the trees. The cool scent of autumn in the air and the sun on my face—it was a beautiful day.

The world was hard. The world was amazing.

I arrived at school in the middle of lunch and headed for the cafeteria. I smelled the menu before I saw it: King Ranch chicken with green beans, brownie for dessert—mouth-watering heaven.

I got my tray and settled in a corner, as far from everyone else as I could get. Before I could take the first bite, Amy sat down beside me in a wave of amber and vanilla and anxiety. No tray, so she'd already eaten.

She took my hand under the table. "What's wrong?"

I'll tell you later had worn thin. I couldn't think of a good lie, and the truth had been out of the question. It was time for that to change, and not just because she had my back when her friends were ready to destroy me. Not because she didn't give a damn what they thought about me—or about her. Or because it felt good to have someone I liked, someone like her, believe in me. I needed to tell her the truth because I needed to be worthy of being believed. I needed to tell her because she needed to know the danger in continuing to stand with me.

I glanced away for a second. Met Rude's gaze across the crowded, cavernous room.

He read the intention written on my face and considered. Shrugged.

Amy squeezed my hand. "What am I missing?"

"Let's go outside," I said.

CHAPTER 25

I LED HER TO the quietest place out back, far enough away from the skater's island that we wouldn't be overheard unless she cursed me out at the top of her lungs. The sun shone like a spotlight, the kind used for interrogations. The wind gusted, lifting the blue-black fire of Amy's hair. We sat on the grass. I breathed in the perfume of cool earth and talked.

Her dark eyes grew flintier by the second. Her cheeks reddened.

"You're shitting me, Kevin Landon."

"Why would I do that?" A rational question that invited a rational response.

She balled her hands into fists. "Because you want to get rid of me. Because you want to make a fool out of me. You could've just told me there's another girl instead of making up this BS story."

"What other girl?" It took me a second—a second too long—to snap that she must mean Simone.

"God, Kevin. To think I told Britt and Zoe they were assholes for saying what they did about you. I defended you. I made my costume for the party tomorrow night. I even started on yours."

"But the bus girl is—"

"A half-human, half-faery. Right. Please, Kevin, make up a good lie next time."

"I don't like her like that, Amy." That, right there, was the first and only lie I'd told, and I didn't even understand that until I tasted the words on my tongue.

How did I feel about Simone? Confused and awed came close, but they didn't cut it.

"But she likes you."

I couldn't deny that. That would be another lie.

"Go to hell, Kevin." She stood, all elbows and knees.

She didn't understand, and I didn't know how to make her—I only knew I didn't want her to go. I grabbed for her arm. "Wait—"

She swung at me and struck gold. Her fist slammed into my nose.

A sharp, sickening spike of pain bowled me over. I covered my face with my hands. Felt something sticky at the same time as I tasted blood.

"Don't touch me, Kevin."

I watched her go, blood dripping down my chin, until she disappeared around a corner. Only then did I notice the people staring. They hadn't heard a word we'd said, but they'd seen the punch, and the blood was undeniable.

One of the staring people? Scott. Who came right over and butted in when all I wanted to do was find a place to hide.

He carried his phone in one hand and an iced coffee in the other. He sipped casually, looking from me to Amy's rapid retreat and back again. "Jeez, Kev. What'd you say to her?"

As if he were my friend. "You don't get to ask me anything."

"I deserve that."

"Yeah, you do. Go away, man."

I needed a wad of paper towels to soak up the blood, and I needed them fast. It was either that or my shirt—which was already splattered. I tilted my head back and saw stars.

"Is it broken?" Scott asked.

"What do you care?"

Scott shoved his hands in his pockets. "You look like you're in trouble, Kev."

"I've *been* in trouble, man. You didn't give a crap before, so why should you now?"

"That's not fair."

"What the fuck is fair? We've been friends a long time. You blew me off like someone you met last week. What do you want?"

"To say I'm sorry. To make it right."

How did you make something like that right? A half hour ago, I'd have sworn you couldn't. Scott picked now to tell me this? *Now?*

"You've got a helluva lot of balls."

"More than I've got brains," Scott said.

"Can't trust you."

"Don't blame you. But try me if you're game. Tell me what's going on."

"So you can what?"

"Help," he said.

That could backfire with serious repercussions, like with Amy. Did I care anymore?

I told the story again, this time without mincing on details or tiptoeing around the blood and guts, holding back only how I felt about Simone. Scott interrupted me with the occasional question. The bell rang, but he didn't make any attempt to head to class. He didn't even fidget.

Scott picked a handful of grass and let it fly into the wind. "I want in."

I squinted at him. "You believe me?"

"I've known you since forever, Kev. You'd never make up something like this. You don't have that kind of imagination."

I couldn't decide whether to be offended.

"Don't mean it like that," he said.

"Like what?"

"Like however it's written all over your face. I just mean you're pretty literal. Practical. You have too much to deal with on the daily to get fantastical. So, if you say this is happening, no matter how it sounds, it must be happening. And Rude is—I don't know." The corners of Scott's mouth turned down. "I could kick his ass for the way he put me down at the party, but if it hadn't been for him—and you—something worse could've happened."

He could've driven out of there drunk and hurt someone. Killed someone. Like my mom.

He didn't say those words, but he thought them. I didn't have to hear the words in my mind to know it. It wasn't an apology. Scott didn't do apologies. Whether I took it as one anyway depended on what he chose to do now.

"What's the plan?" he asked again.

"Told you everything I know."

"What can I do?" Scott asked.

"Be available."

Scott nodded. "I wish I could say you can stay with me if you need to. Dad would go off like a bomb."

"That's all right, man. Even if he said it was cool, I don't think I could deal with him tonight."

Scott grinned wryly. "One dad at a time."

"Exactly. Keep your phone on."

"Will do."

Would he really? Only one way to find out.

We parted ways once we got into the building. Scott headed upstairs for his class. I hesitated in the hall, shifting my weight from one foot to the other.

Go see the nurse? I had a bloody excuse for that. I knew without having looked in the mirror that I resembled someone out of a horror movie, but, for once, nobody stared—because everyone was in class.

I had questions. I could visit the nurse or I could go after the answers.

CHAPTER 26

THE SECRETARY IN THE front office had stepped out and Nance had someone with him when I arrived. I barged in, not surprised to see that, amid the stacks of files and papers and the dusty bookcase with the thirsty ivy, the counselor was talking to Stacy. The way he leaned forward, elbows on the desk, with no file open and no official documents, said *personal conversation* to me.

"Sorry to interrupt," I said, aware that I sounded anything but.

Nance leaned back in his chair. "Stacy, would you excuse us?"

She shrugged. And gave me a look of supreme understanding as she left and shut the door behind her. It was presumptuous and embarrassing.

"Sit down, Mr. Landon."

"Don't feel like it."

Nance gestured toward the chair Stacy had just vacated. "You don't have much left in you, either. Sit down or fall down. Your choice."

I stayed on my feet. "Thanks for writing those notes earlier. For sending Rude to my house."

"You're welcome, Kevin."

"Here's the thing: Why'd you do it?"

Nance opened a drawer in his desk and pulled out a bottled water and a wad of paper towels. He offered them to me. "You want to clean up?"

"Is that your final answer?"

"I understand you're frustrated, Kevin."

Damn right. "Stop saying my name like you're trying to calm me down."

"I'm offending you?"

Of all the people who'd offended me in the last week, Mr. Nance was low on the list. "No. It just won't work."

I looked at the water and towels in his hands. The blood streaking my face and crusting under my nose felt itchy and awful. I took what Nance offered.

"You got a mirror?" I asked.

He opened the drawer again and produced a large hand mirror. "Will this do?"

I nodded and took it.

He set his hands on the desk and laced his fingers together. "I expected you to come with questions. I'm just not sure I know how to answer them."

"Truthfully would be good."

Worry etched Nance's brow.

"If you're thinking I won't believe you, stop," I said.

"Very well, Kev—very well. When you were here the other day, I told you that once upon a time I'd been just like you. That's more true than you realize."

Sure. Right. "Why did you write the notes and send Rude?"

"I'm not in the habit of dreaming about my charges, but I had a dream last night that was so vivid it could've been real. I knew you were in trouble. I knew I had to send Mr. Davies to help you."

A dream? A true dream? A week ago, I'd have laughed. "What's that, like, prophecy?"

"More like communication."

"From?"

"My daughter. I only hear from her at this time of year." His eyes welled with tears, but he didn't shed them. "She's been gone for seven years. Unsolved disappearance. The police expect she's dead. They told me I needed to prepare myself for that possibility a long time ago. But I know better."

His daughter. Talked to him in dreams. The world was truly bigger and weirder than I'd ever thought. I couldn't be sure about anything anymore. I shifted my weight from one foot to the other.

"She was a singer, my daughter."

I gripped the chairback in front of me. "What's her name?"

"What does it matter? She goes by another now, but then I suspect you already know that."

He was right. I could sit down or fall down. I took the chair and glanced up and behind him, needing a minute before I had to meet his gaze, to see the pain in his eyes.

The oil painting behind his desk, the one of the Wild Hunt, included a pretty good likeness of the actual Faery King at its head. No, more than pretty good. The detail was exact.

"You paint that?"

"My daughter did, before she left home one evening and never returned. May I ask you something?"

I nodded, afraid of what he might say.

"Is she all right?"

None of us were. "She's been in Faery so long she's grown wings."

"I've seen them in my dreams."

"She's changing. Becoming one of them. She's still...solid—flesh and bones and blood. But eventually, she'll have a body made of light. That's what I'm told."

"By whom?"

Had I said too much? Nance had to know already—or at least suspect—didn't he? "Rude."

"Mr. Davies is in a unique position." Nance took a deep breath. "Is there a way to help her?"

"I don't know."

"Are you trying?"

I wanted to. That I didn't know how was a source of shame. "She's been helping me. I'd be in worse trouble without her, and maybe I still am. She told me how to get the Faery King to let my father go, except it's impossible."

"All the great heroic tasks are."

"What?"

"You should take some mythology when you get to college, Mr. Landon." Nance rose and walked around the desk, perched on the chair beside mine. "Can you take me to her?"

Didn't he know where she was? How to get there on his own? If he didn't, why not?

"I can see the questions in your eyes. The answer is, it's complicated."

I understood complicated. "I could get you there, yeah. But I couldn't let you in. Only she can do that."

"Those are the rules."

"In my experience."

"Just so." Nance glanced down at his dress shoes.

I didn't know anything about his relationship with Simone. Whether they got along. Whether they hated each other. The guy was clearly hurting.

"I think you should have your nose looked at, Mr. Landon. And why don't you find Mr. Davies after school and meet me in the faculty parking lot? I drive a Cadillac. 1969."

I had no idea what that meant, other than that the car was older than me. "I can't be seen with Rude right now. I can't be seen with your daughter, and probably not with you either."

"Tell me why."

I took a deep breath and spat out the story for a third time, abbreviated version. He didn't seem the least bit surprised by any of it.

"I'll do what I can to help," he said.

I didn't know what that might be. Maybe it would make a difference. Maybe not. "If you want to visit your daughter, Rude will have to take you. You should be careful."

"I'm not afraid of the King."

"You should be."

"If it comes down to it, I'm not afraid to die, Kevin. The only thing I'm afraid of is fear."

"The only thing we have to fear is fear itself?"

His lips curved. "You should be on your way."

Just like that, I ended up out in the hall again, face mostly clean but shirt still looking like it'd taken a bloodbath.

Simone was Nance's daughter. Simone was somebody's kid. Seven years missing.

The secretary was back in the front office. She peered at me through her rhinestone bifocals. I smiled at her half-heartedly. She frowned. I knew exactly what she saw: a bloodied, battered trouble-maker who might be arrested any day. Someone who deserved what he got.

I went to bathroom and changed my shirt for a clean one from my pack, tossing the stained one in the trash. I barely recognized the reflection in the mirror. Swollen nose I expected, but the haunted look in my eyes? The downturned corners of my mouth?

I'd thought I could go through the motions of my day, but that hadn't turned out so well. Hours to go before I could get out of here, and I had a lot of thinking to do. I'd have to do it in class. I'd have to make it work.

I was cornered. There had to be a way out.

CHAPTER 27

I BROKE INTO Nance's office after hours. No witnesses in the hall to see me do it. If a security camera had caught me—if anyone monitored the cameras—a guard would be on my ass within ten minutes and I'd be in even more trouble. But I couldn't care about that. Nance's office was the only place I could be alone without eyes on my every move.

Without Nance, the office was just another musty room buried in aging paper. The overhead light was off, but the desk lamp glowed bright. The painted image of the King on the wall looked at me as if I were prey. In the emptiness, he seemed larger. More solid. More threatening.

"Fuck you," I said aloud, the echo of my voice turning my skin to gooseflesh.

I'd never hated anyone in my entire life, not even the drunk driver who'd killed my mom. But I hated him. The rush of it invigorated, flushing my face and making my heart race.

Every thought I'd had over the last three hours had been about him. I'd turned the situation over and over again, looking for that way out. Looking for a weakness. I'd only ended up with more questions.

One question, specifically, that only one person I knew might be able to answer.

I turned my back on the painting and closed my eyes, taking deep breaths until I calmed. I felt the weight of my feet on the floor, the warm air blowing from the vent above the door. My heartbeat slowed. I called the image of Simone's face into my mind in painstaking detail.

Violet-blue eyes. Red hair, streaked with purple. Every angle and every curve. The points of her teeth.

This time of day in my world, she was in Faery. She wouldn't arrive in the alley until midnight, and I couldn't go to her. But she could come to me.

I whispered her name. It hung in the air, thick and heavy. Minutes passed. Dust motes floated in and out of the desk lamp's halo. Time stretched like a rubber band, the space between heartbeats lengthening until my heart seemed to barely beat at all.

In the hush, a pinpoint of light appeared in the far, dark corner. It grew into a jagged line, a tear in the air, widening in fits and starts as if someone had grabbed the edges in their hands and ripped them apart.

Light so bright it blinded blasted from the other side of the rift. I raised an arm to shield my eyes, but couldn't look away.

On the other side of the opening, I could just barely make out a swath of green. The dense tops of trees. I sucked in a breath and tasted rich, rain-drenched earth. The air shimmered silver and gold, as if threads of precious metal had been woven through oxygen and carbon dioxide. A low-level buzz, like a million faraway bees, rose like a wave.

Then the doorway closed, and all that remained was the brightness. My eyes adjusted just enough so that I could gaze directly at it. No, not it. Her.

Simone shone like a star. An unstable one. About to go nova.

Her voice rang, like bells. She sounded surprised. "You called my name."

"And you came, like you said you would. Can you turn down the glow?"

She shook her head.

"Is this how you look when you're in Faery?"

"No, Kevin. It's new."

"It's beautiful."

She smiled, but the expression didn't reach her eyes. Something was wrong. She was turning. Becoming all the way fae.

"It's not what you think," she said.

"You're not losing the rest of your humanity?"

She walked toward me, the tips of her wings flickering like flames. The closer she came, the easier it became to see that the shining originated in her chest. In her heart. It was beautiful. It was terrifying.

"What is that?"

"My magic," she said. "That's where it lives, you know. Where it comes from. You understand?"

"The magic in me comes from my heart?"

She nodded. "It's part of who you are, Kevin."

I couldn't believe that. The powers that'd come on suddenly weren't something I'd done, they'd been done to me.

She reached for me. I flinched before she touched, certain the light would burn, but it didn't. It felt cool to the touch as she took my hands in hers.

"Kevin, I need you to listen to me closely. I need you to hear me, because I don't have a lot of time left, and neither do you. It's Halloween now. The King knows about the decision you made, and he'll come for you with his Hunt. You have only a handful of hours."

I shook my head. "That's tomorrow."

"Not anymore. Time—"

Time had shifted again, like it had in the King's presence, the world turning in what felt to me like only minutes. And she said that the King knew I'd refused the spell of forgetting.

"He knows because—"

"You called my name."

How could he hear? How could he know? Because he was the goddamn King of Faery, and she was his subject, and he'd been watching her and me, all of us. There was nowhere to run. Nowhere I could hide.

"I didn't know that would happen."

"You couldn't. And I didn't think to tell you. Remember, fae can see the future—many possible futures—because the magic that infuses your world with beauty flows through our world first. We can guess what will happen before it comes to pass here. But the ultimate choices? Those belong to humans. They belong to you."

I knew this was important. I couldn't wrap my head around it. It was overwhelming.

"Why did you call me, Kevin?"

"Because I'm trying to find a way through. Because I need to know why the King won't just kill me. He's holding my dad hostage to my good behavior, but if I were dead, he wouldn't have to do that. I don't understand why he doesn't just off us both. There has to be a reason, and it has to be important. A clue for how to survive. A tool I can use. Something."

She swallowed hard. "Are you asking me that question?"

I met her gaze. "Yes."

"Then ask it."

She meant I had to ask directly. Not sideways. Not vaguely. She was the lock. My question was the key.

"Why won't the King kill me?"

She closed her eyes, a wave of peace crossing her face. I'd never seen anything like it, relief so palpable I could reach out and touch it—and did. I loosened my hands from her grip and lifted them to cup her shining face.

"He won't kill you because you are important to Faery. To the realm. Without you, the realm dies."

If I thought what she'd said before was hard to grasp, this was beyond extra. "Why doesn't he want me to remember who and what I am—to remember you and Rude?"

"You may be necessary for Faery to survive, but you're dangerous to him personally."

To a being that powerful? Someone who could see the future and hear thoughts and heaven only knew what else? "That's impossible."

"He's not invulnerable, Kevin. He's not all-knowing and all-seeing."

"Neither am I."

She thought for a moment. "I told you these things because you asked the right question. I know them in the first place because I'm a singer, not just in the human world, but in Faery. Being a singer—it means the same thing in both places. I draw on my own emotions and sing them into being, spinning them like a spell. I read the emotions of those who listen and weave them into the spell. It's a symbiosis. In the human world, I can sing about anything at all—love, hate, war, peace, a million wrongs, a million rights. In Faery, I sing about history and prophecy."

"For him."

She nodded. "For the King."

I began to understand the position she was in, to imagine the kind of rules she had to follow. To understand that she couldn't break them, but she could bend the hell out of them.

She'd given me valuable information. I only hoped that, when the time came, I would know how to use it.

She held my gaze. "Kevin, do you remember when I told you my name? Do you remember what you traded me for that privilege?"

How could I forget? "You asked for one night of my life."

"This is it."

I braced myself. What would she ask me to do? What—

"It won't hurt you."

"You said that before. Back at the bus, when we met."

"I did. You asked before whether I was losing the last of my humanity."

"You didn't answer." I tilted her chin so I could look her in the eye. "You are, aren't you?"

"It's my choice."

"But I know how much that scares you. Why would you choose that?"

"To help you."

"No—I'm supposed to help you."

She set her hands on top of mine. "Kevin, right now there's nothing you can do to make things better for me. The King has you trapped. Your powers are new, and you don't know how to use them yet."

"Are you saying you don't trust me?"

"Trust has nothing to do with it—but, yes, I trust you. I believe in you. But facts are facts. Nothing is going to stop my slide into Faery."

"You don't know that."

"Yes, I do. There's no scenario in which it changes. The fae part of me acknowledges that. My only choices are whether I continue to fight it and the inevitable happens slowly, or whether I take the power I've been using to fight and do something good with it instead. That something good is you."

I shook my head. "I can't let you do this."

Her cheeks flushed an angry red. "You know that saving the people you love could mean giving your life for them."

"I—"

She interrupted. "Don't deny it. I feel it in you. The determination. The sacrifice already made. You're willing to die if it comes to that."

"I don't want anyone to get hurt because of me."

"There's a word missing from that sentence."

I filled it in: I didn't want anyone *else* to get hurt because of me.

"Your mother's death and what your father did afterwards are not your fault, Kevin."

Her words rocked me like a slap. "I've never said they were."

"You don't have to."

"Because you can feel it in me."

She nodded.

"You don't get to tell me how I feel."

The anger drained out of her and seemed to find a way into me. I needed to take my hands off of her, to take a step back. All I wanted to do was scream. Run. Be anywhere but here. But she rested her hands on top of mine, and when I tried to pull away, she refused to let me.

"How is it your fault?"

I pressed my lips into a thin line. She didn't get to tell me how I felt. She didn't get to ask questions like that. Having supernatural emotional insight didn't give her the right to act as if she knew me.

We hadn't spent time together. We'd never talked about the everyday stuff that allowed us to get to know each other. We'd met because of a crisis, and life-or-death was all we had in common.

Except for the way she made me feel with her magic. Her presence. Her touch.

She knew how I felt. She would know it if I lied. I didn't want to disappoint her—not now, when the end of life as I knew it loomed large. Lying to her would be bad, but just as bad? Lying to myself. If I had to be one-hundred-percent honest, if I had to strip myself to the quick, I could do that with her in a way I'd never been able to do with anyone else.

I took a deep breath and blew it out slowly. My voice shook. "I'm not enough."

The words hung in the air, poisonous and sharp. They didn't make sense in the heart-light that shone from Simone's skin. They rang false. They fell apart like burnt paper in a high wind. Like ashes.

"I'm here to tell you that you are, Kevin. You're enough."

I closed my eyes tight enough to see stars. If I didn't look at her, I wouldn't fall apart. I couldn't—I had to stay solid. Stay strong. Be ready. Because my world was ending. Because people needed me.

"Strength means knowing when to ask for help," she said. "And to do that, you have to believe you're worth it—or you have to be willing to believe."

I breathed in what she said, the sound of it, the emotion behind it. The truth in it.

"Can you be willing, Kevin?"

I looked at her. She deserved that much and more. I nodded.

"Then you have to be willing to believe that other people think you're worth it."

She leaned into me, brushing her lips against mine. She tasted of roses and starlight and sex. I kissed her back, feeling only her and the magic that flowed through her before she pulled me in closer, heart to heart.

I buried my face in her hair, understanding that there would never be another chance to do that. To be this close. The kiss had meant one thing, and one thing only.

Goodbye.

She spoke softly, her breath warm against my neck. "I give you the last of my humanity in all its messy, beautiful grace and glory. There's so much magic in it. So much magic in the love we carry inside of us. It's up to you to choose how you use it. You'll know how. You have to trust yourself."

I didn't want the gift. I wanted her to stay. I wanted her to be okay.

"Never be afraid to be what you are, Kevin. Never be afraid to be real. To be vulnerable."

Nothing scared me more.

"Promise me."

How could I deny her? "I promise."

The light shining from her grew bigger and brighter, covering me, flowing along my skin. Flowing into me through the pores of my skin, through my breath. It flashed from her heart to mine, pulsing with the rhythm of my heartbeat, infiltrating my blood, shaking me to the core.

Then it was over.

The light winked out—all of it, even the halo of the desk lamp. The office was still and silent and heartbreakingly empty.

Simone was gone.

My phone buzzed. The sound and vibration hurt my ears and skin. My legs couldn't decide whether to hold me.

I staggered to the desk, white-knuckling its edges until my breathing evened out and my heart calmed. Only then did I dare to try to make my fingers move properly, to reach into my pocket. I blinked until my eyes consented to focus, and still it took me a minute to read and make sense of the three numbers that appeared on the screen.

Rude had texted a jumble of characters. Made no sense.

On the heels of that, a thought so loud it threatened to split my head in two.

King here.

I thought hard at him, having no idea whether my power worked like that. *On my way.*

I sucked in a breath, tapping the same message into the screen with clumsy fingers and headed out of the office, heedless of security, head ready to explode and every muscle aching, sneakers squeaking on the floor. I called a car as I pushed the front doors open on creaking hinges. The nearest driver was two minutes away. I confirmed the ride, fidgeting while I waited.

Two minutes was an eternity. The ride to Rude's place was torture.

The door to the pool house hung open on one hinge. Fallen leaves had blown into the entry. The wicker furniture had been tossed around like matchsticks, the lamps knocked over. Broken glass from busted light bulbs glittered on the floor in the dregs of the daylight that filtered through the blinds. The air stank of blood and sulfur. Underneath that, the same starlight I'd tasted on Simone's lips. The only sounds were wind and silence, and a car starting somewhere down the street, engine belts squealing.

I was too late to help. I knew that before I cleared a path to the back room to find the twin bed, where Oscar had been sleeping and healing, empty. Sheets, half-torn off the bed. Items that'd populated the night stand, scattered on the floor and strangely aged—large soda spilled into a half-dried puddle, twenty tissues torn one by one from the box and covered in a layer of dust, remote control for the TV in pieces, batteries corroded and leaking.

The hell?

I texted Rude's. When he didn't answer, I called. His voicemail picked up.

I dialed Scott. That call went to voicemail, too. I waited a minute, expecting a return call or text. Scott had promised to stay available. But he didn't respond. Maybe he'd blown me off. Maybe his whole I'm-sorry-I-care-now routine had been nothing but bullshit, but I didn't believe that. Not in my heart and not in my gut.

I tried Amy's number. No answer.

She had a reason not to answer my calls. She was pissed at me, and

I couldn't blame her in the least, because she was right. But her not answering right here and now? The goose bumps that rose on my skin and the tightening in my belly told me something was wrong.

That the danger that dogged me had found my friends.

Rude's panicked thought. Blood. Sulfur. Starlight.

The King or his henchmen—it didn't matter which—had taken my friends. My father. My friends. Oscar. My not-girlfriend. And Simone would be with him now, too.

Everything I'd feared had just become real.

The King had warned me. Simone had explained why he wouldn't just kill me. Why he both needed and was afraid of me. Still, I hadn't expected this to happen so fast, before I'd even had a chance to figure out a plan.

I stepped outside as the sun set, two-and-a-half hours early by my reckoning, an orange ball of fire on the horizon one second, gone the next—all of it happening so fast, as if I'd walked onto the set of a time-lapse video. Shock wanted to take hold. I fought it.

Faery time had bled into our world, like it had at my house when the King visited, like it had in Nance's office when Simone had arrived. That was the only explanation that made sense.

The water in the pool rippled. Next door, a gate creaked as it opened and closed. From my vantage in the backyard, I could see lights shining in the big house, where the shadows of Rude's parents moved behind drawn sheers, their movements jerky and sped-up. For a handful of seconds, the mouthwatering perfume of pot roast pushed through the air, then became a ghost and faded as if it'd never been at all.

In the space it took to draw a breath, the joyful noise of children's shouts and laughter floated on the breeze. Trick-or-treaters up and down the street, having the time of their lives. Then, as suddenly as it had begun, it was gone.

The settling darkness deepened from gray to indigo to black, the moon rising overhead as if someone pulled it on a string. The air pressed against my skin, heavy with anticipation.

My rational mind couldn't get a grip. The magic within me could and did, though. It found solid footing. It rang like a bell inside my heart. It *sang*. It knew what was going down.

The King and his Wild Hunt were riding. Taking my friends because I'd refused the King's offer. Upping the ante. Making sure I drank the tea. That I did as I was told before others faced the consequences of my actions.

If I got in line and stayed there, I had no guarantee from the King that he would let my people go. He could keep them forever. He could do whatever he wanted to with them. And I, having forgotten all about them, would have abandoned them to whatever fate he chose for them.

I knew because the magic inside told me that I wasn't the first person he'd done this to, and if I didn't stop him, I wouldn't be the last.

Simone had given me a priceless gift. I couldn't allow her trust in me to be in vain.

Fuck the King. Fuck Faery politics and cosmic forces and cosmic threats. He wasn't playing. Neither would I.

All I needed was a way in.

The only people who could help me with that were gone. I had no way to call the King, and he had no reason to come. I could think of only one chance. One break. But only if I could get there quickly enough.

I ran back into the trashed pool house and collected the keys to Rude's Explorer. I rolled out of the driveway as Mr. and Mrs. Davies turned out the light in their bedroom and lay down to sleep.

The traffic on the freeway sped past me in ribbons of golden and red light. I punched the gas, coaxing every last bit of speed out of the engine, taking corners too fast, praying I wouldn't get pulled over. Praying for time to run in my favor.

I pulled into the alley at midnight, just as the bus shimmered into the human world, lights twinkling in its lowered windows. I scrambled out of the Explorer, kicking an empty beer bottle out of my way as I rushed the door without a clue as to how I would get in without Simone to grant me access.

But the moment my hand touched the door, a light flared in my chest, and the mechanism opened the door. I climbed inside, leaning against the dash, wrapping the fingers of one hand around the steering wheel.

It took only one second to see that the bus was empty. That everything Simone had kept inside, everything that had made it hers, was gone. The oil paintings. The clothes. The patchouli incense. The feel of her.

At two seconds, the bus seemed to shrink. To grow narrow and tall like a funhouse mirror, the space inside compressed and pressed against my body. I tried to draw a breath. Couldn't expand my lungs. Couldn't move a muscle.

Three seconds, the air turned to fire. I tasted nothing but sulfur.

Outside the windows, brick and asphalt, moon and stars spun, fast and wild. The bus vanished from the human world, taking me with it.

CHAPTER 28

T HE BUS CAME to rest in the middle of a forest, at the foot of a tree with a trunk so massive, I couldn't see anything but bark from my vantage by the steering wheel. I could finally breathe, move. My eyebrows and nose hairs felt singed. I could still taste sulfur, but the nastiness faded with every passing moment. I levered open the door and peered out.

The air hit me like a tidal wave of sweetness so hard and deep, tears welled in my eyes. It smelled the way air was supposed to smell, laden with layers of thick loam and sap and green, growing things. And, somewhere nearby, water. The enormous tree looked like some kind of fir. Not a pine, like at home, but a close relative. The trees around it, in every direction, were all different. Oak, ash, hawthorn. Apple, cherry, fig. I had no idea how I knew all that. I'd never seen a hawthorn tree in my life.

This was the place Simone returned to every night? This didn't seem anything like her. It didn't seem like anything or anyone I'd ever known.

My hackles rose.

Someone was watching. Someone knew I'd come. And that

someone even now reported my presence to the King. I didn't know how I knew that, either.

Nowhere to go but out.

I descended the steps, my feet sinking into the soil that seemed to have a mind of its own—it knew me, who I was, where I'd come from. It rose underfoot at an angle that propelled me away from the bus. I took the step forward it wanted me to, and then another. I glanced at my feet and then looked up again—to find that the trees had moved.

I blinked, expecting my vision to refocus. For things to go back to the way they'd been only a second ago. Didn't happen.

The trees were literally in different places than they'd been before. Their new configuration formed a single path leading in only one direction. The same one the earth itself had encouraged me to walk.

I took a single step onto the path, twigs crackling underfoot, and the forest undulated like a heat wave over hot asphalt. My head spun, and no amount of blinking fixed the picture this time either. I knelt, hoping the ground beneath me stayed solid. That it would carry me through whatever magic filled the air. I dug my fingers into the dirt. Grabbed on to tree roots and held on for dear life until the world stilled.

I crouched before an ornately wrought gate. Iron? Steel? Silver? It was so covered in dirt and age, I couldn't tell. On the other side of the gate, a couple of stone steps led down to a stone door.

The King was behind that door. So were my people.

I reached up, half-expecting the gate to transform or disappear, but when I wrapped my fingers around the latch, it only opened.

A crow's caw echoed above me. I didn't glance up. I didn't dare look at anything except where I wanted to go. I duck-walked through the gate, sliding down the stairs. I laid hands on the door, stone rough against my palms.

The light in my heart flashed as it had in the alley. The door swung inward, revealing total darkness. I couldn't make out curves or edges or enemies. I stuck out my hand, half-expecting it to get chopped off or grabbed. It stayed attached and no one pulled me forward, but I couldn't see it inside the inky blackness. It was as if my arm ended at the wrist.

The animal part of me, the part that knew I was being watched, refused to walk into that. The fear that rose from the pit of my belly felt primal. This was more than danger. If I entered that darkness, I'd never be the same. I might not even be me anymore.

The magic inside me agreed.

I couldn't let that matter. I had one job to do. One purpose. One foot in front of the other. Eyes on the prize.

I took the next step.

There was no floor, nothing to catch me. My stomach flipped and dipped and ended up somewhere in the vicinity of my throat. I waited to fall. It didn't happen.

Muffled footfalls echoed up ahead. And voices. The clink of glasses. The scrape of silverware on plates. The perfume of roast pork and potatoes. The stink of fear—not my own.

Shapes formed in the darkness: an arched doorway, this one made out of wood, carved along the edges with spiraling snakes. I felt stone underfoot, something solid to hold on to, like I'd done outside when the forest shifted. As I took another step forward, the rest of the space took solid form.

A dog stood guard beneath the arch. Only it was too big to be a dog, and it had gray fur and huge paws. And the cold intelligence in its eyes? Definitely not domesticated. It watched me for a moment before angling its head as a sign that I should pass.

I swallowed hard and moved through and into a torch-lined corridor, the light faint at first but growing stronger by the second. Doors were set into the walls every few feet. Just looking at them made me queasy. None of them were for me.

The hall opened out into a dining room big enough to hold hundreds of people. At the moment, it contained only a few:

Dad, dressed in his black-and-white striped pajamas, a glass of wine in his trembling hand. Rude, whose cheeks flushed the same angry orange as his hair. Oscar leaned against him, eyes at half-mast.

Scott sat beside Amy, both of them pale and shell-shocked. All of them sat at a long, rectangular table.

The King sat not at the head of the table, but at its center. All the seats were occupied except the one to his right, between himself and Rude. The King outshone everyone else at the table but one, the woman on his left.

She gazed at me with eyes full of stars. Her blue-black hair cascaded in luscious waves down to the middle of her back, contrasted against skin so fair, it was nearly translucent, the same as Simone's. The Queen's mouth, wine-red and intoxicating just to look at, curved. She wore a dress of the same red that hugged her every curve. She smiled at me, showing razor-sharp teeth.

She, not the King, presided over the table and the court.

The King rose. "The guest of honor."

He meant for me to join him. To take the empty seat beside him. I didn't know what else to do, so I made my way over, conscious of my friends' and my father's eyes on me. Of the hope in them.

The King and Queen watched, too, eyes narrowed and calculating.

They weren't the only ones. I'd thought the room was empty because it looked that way. But as I marched down the center of the space, from the corner of my eye I saw that the room was much, much larger than I'd originally reckoned. That tables just like the King's and Queen's filled the place, every seat taken by beings out of dreams and nightmares.

Creatures made from shadows. Men with the faces of stags, wearing crowns of antlers. Women whose clothes dripped water or seemed to be made from living butterflies. People who seemed to be neither gender—or both. Horses made of ice and fire. Every step, a new wonder. Every footfall, a new terror.

When I finally reached my destination, I saw that all the food had been eaten, that all the wine had been drunk. That it'd taken me at least an hour to cross the dining hall. That the King had placed his foot in the chair he'd offered me.

"You have brass balls," he said. "You're just like your father. You don't listen."

I was nothing like my dad. I didn't want to be anything like him. I'd never leave my kid to handle everything dropped on me after Mom died.

I looked at Dad, praying to see some semblance of the man he'd once been. Something in him that hadn't been beaten down or drowned in beer or fae poisons. He met my gaze with every feeling in his heart showing naked and plain on his face. He would never be that man again. He was only who he'd become. Broken. Flawed. Human.

It didn't matter what I wished for, only what was. Could I accept that?

Simone's words echoed inside my head. *Humanity has its own magic.* I wished to hell I knew what she'd meant, but right now the only thing that mattered was what it meant to me.

"I'm here for them," I said. "All of them. Are we going to do this—whatever it is—here and now?"

"We are," the King said. "This fight isn't just about me, Kevin. It involves the future of my people. It's only fitting that it be done in their presence."

No lie, I felt rattled by the audience. Anybody would've. Any *human* would've.

The King met and held my gaze. A heartbeat later, a punch of magic struck me in the side of the head, slicing its way through my skull and into my mind. I tried to call out. To struggle. To push it away. The magic held me still. It turned my sight inward.

The King and Queen, my father, my friends, all faded. I could see only the workings of my own mind, wrapped in threads of gold and silver energy that could only belong to the King. My own magic, the deep green of leaves after a hard rain, pulsed and fought, but couldn't break free. The King had control, and nothing I could do would make him let go.

He reached for my memories, searching, seizing. Following a trail. From my first glimpse of Faery through the door of the bus to the last moment I'd spent in Simone's arms before she'd exploded in light, from the moment I'd met him in the kitchen while my father slept to the sound of Simone's voice as she sang and the wildness she'd made me feel. Sitting across the table from Oscar at the restaurant, listening to him tell me about magic and fairies and thinking the guy had to be out of his mind. The party at Rude's, the second Scott's thoughts had speared into my mind. The awe. The confusion. The fear.

Still, the King reached back, rifling through embarrassment and determination and grief, until he found what he was looking for. The memory stuttered and started to play from the beginning, but not as if I were watching it on a screen.

I was in it. I was there. I was—

CHAPTER 29

THE SOUND OF the storm woke me. Rain splattered the windows, falling like bullets on the ash tree and the driveway outside. Flash of lighting. Roll of thunder so loud, it rattled the glass.

I opened my eyes to slits and reached for my phone. The face lit up, clock reading 2:45 a.m. I rolled over, tangling my legs in the sheets, and threw an arm across my eyes like a vampire afraid of the sun. The harsh glare of the porch light poured into the room through the slats of the window blinds. Which could only mean Mom hadn't made it home yet.

Weird, because whenever she hit the town with her girls she always stumbled in around one.

The doorbell rang.

For a second, my muzzy brain didn't recognize the sound. Then it finally snapped to. Mom had forgotten her keys. I peeled myself out of bed and pulled on a pair of jeans on the way, tripping over trying to slide my feet into the pants legs and banging into the walls in the hall. When I opened the door to find two cops on the stoop, I blinked at them, not understanding, until the one with the dark hair and the beard asked whether my dad was home and a bomb full of fear detonated in my gut and my chest.

Dad came up behind me. He was always slower, waking up. His face bleached white at the sight of the cops. He refused to let them come in, because if they didn't set foot inside, if they didn't tell him what they'd come to say, then it wouldn't be true.

I refused to hear the words they spoke, shaking my head, but the meaning slipped in anyway, an arrow through my heart. I couldn't breathe. I couldn't stand there. I couldn't—

I slammed open the door, slipped on the slick porch and went down, scraping my palms and skinning my knees. Scrambled to my feet and careened off the whisky barrel where Mom had planted lilies (would never plant them again) and raced across the lawn, past the cruiser, into the street. Into the puddled light of the streetlamp.

The sky opened up completely. Wind gusted, blowing the shadows of branches across the lamplight, plunging me into the dark. The cold, hard rain soaked me to the skin, all the way to the marrow. My legs gave way, dropping me to the asphalt. I huddled there, shivering. Screaming.

The sound echoed in my head. In my heart.

The King examined it as if it were an insect, then moved on, uprooting me from the rain-drenched street as he forged a path deeper into my memory. Searching. Reaching.

He was looking for something worse. I knew it instinctively. The magic in me knew it as sure as the sun in the human world would rise in the east. The King wanted to break me. If he couldn't threaten me into forgetting, then he would make me forget, and he would hurt me badly enough that I would never even think about coming back at him.

The King dove deep, head-first into a memory I thought I'd locked away.

Six months after the terrible night on the street, I'd walked into my room after an impossible day of pop quizzes and pull-ups, dumped my backpack on the bed, and realized that the space felt different. Smelled wrong. Sterile.

Not just my room, but the entire house. Something had felt off. Now I understood why.

The warmth had been stolen from it. Everything that reminded me of Mom, everything that she'd given me or that I'd taken after she—well, after—had been stripped away. The spicy scent of her perfume had been literally scrubbed. All that remained was the stink of antiseptic cleaner.

Mom's orange knitted hat and scarf from the coat closet. The yellow sneakers she'd toed off and kicked under the couch. The bowl of fruit still life she painted at her art class. Her collection of cloisonné owls from the garden window.

The photo I kept on my night table, the one of Mom and I in the backyard, her arms around me. She had on her favorite sweater, the ivory cable knit that I'd picked out for her birthday to make sure she got something good, because her birthday was two days before Christmas. I'd been seven.

Mom at the beach, having waded out to her knees and turned around to wave. The waves rolled in slow, dusting the sand with foam. The water sparkled. So did the happiness in his mother's eyes. She swam out with me later. Body-surfed back in.

We'd found a sand dollar on the beach. It had a nick in the side. She said that made it magic. She twirled it in her fingers and made it disappear.

I'd been ten years old.

Dad had no right to take those pictures. No right.

I yelled, hands curling into fists. Pounded on Dad's bedroom door. He didn't answer, just turned up the volume on the TV. I tried the door—locked.

I thought for a split second about calling Scott or Rude. Or just plain leaving. Except I hadn't looked in any of my drawers, and I'd hidden one very important thing in a closet drawer. I hurried down the hall, searching with growing panic for the small box carefully wrapped in waxy, red paper and enough tape to secure Fort Knox, because if Kate Landon wrapped something, it would by God stay that way. The box had a card that went with it, all of it tied together six ways to Sunday with white ribbon, the kind you shredded and curled with a scissors.

In that box was my Christmas gift, the one she'd got months early and would never get around to giving me because she was dead. And I hadn't been able to bring myself to open it either. So I'd stalled. Wait for the right day, the right time, but Christmas had come and gone, and now the act of opening it felt wrong, because opening it meant acknowledging that she was really, truly gone. That she wasn't coming back. That there was no alternate universe where things would ever be different. The box was gone.

Dad cranked the volume on the TV again. I could hear every word of the international news. None of it was good.

I stepped back into the hall. Reached. Pulled the string on the staircase that led to the attic and climbed.

Everything had been packed in brown cardboard file boxes. No labels. No way to tell what they held unless I went through every single one.

I had to walk on my knees for the most part until I came to the center of the space, where the roof peaked and I could stand in a crouch. That would make me clumsy. Dust coated nearly everything. That would make me cough and sneeze.

If Dad heard—and he might, even with the sound up so loud—he'd storm up here. Maybe he'd even throw the boxes away. If he did that, I didn't know how I'd react. What I'd say. What I'd do.

A voice rang inside my head.

Careful, Kevin. Things will get worse. There's no stopping that now. But you can be careful. You can be kind.

Those were not my words. Not my thoughts. Not my voice.

It sounded familiar in a way that cracked open my aching, angry heart. The voice belonged to my mother.

I froze, breathing in the dust and must, one-hundred-percent certain my mind was breaking along with my heart. The voice didn't say anything else. Relief washed through me before a small, quiet thought captured all of my attention, lighting a slow burn of fear.

What if that really had been my mother? What if she'd found a way to talk to me from wherever she was now?

What if that had been the only time—the last time?

"Mom?"

The word faded into the air. No one answered.

I took a deep breath and blew it out slowly, going to work on the boxes. The first box and the second and the third? All clothes, none of them Mom's. But when I lifted the next cardboard lid, I caught a nose full of spice. Mom's perfume. The scent immediately soaked the air. Stuck to my skin where I brushed my fingers over a pair of her jeans or a T-shirt.

The next boxes, papers. Her sketches from the art class. A twine-tied bunch of letters from Dad. Her passport. Her high school diploma. The evidence of a life. How could all of these things that had been hers—how could they become just…things?

I found my Christmas gift among a box of pictures. Right about the time Dad's first footfall sounded on the stairs.

Our eyes met. He stared at me, face flushed, growing redder by the second until he looked as if he'd explode in a ball of rage and fire.

Without a word, he moved, methodically closing the boxes I'd opened, shoving them back into place, closing the distance between us. He did it all bent over. He was taller than me. Bigger.

I stuck the gift box in my pocket. Slid the card down the back of my jeans.

"Give it over, Kevin."

I shook my head.

"I'm not going to ask you again."

"You want to forget her, go ahead. You can't make me forget her, too."

He punched me. Right hook to the side of the head.

My head rocked, and I staggered sideways.

He threw another jab—this time, I got my hand up to block. To grab his arm and push him back.

I spoke through gritted teeth. "Stop."

He didn't seem to hear. He trained his gaze on my pocket and lunged.

I pushed him again, harder. He lost his footing and went down. Stayed down.

I'd never seen him cry. Not even at the funeral.

Dad wrapped his fingers around my ankle and sobbed. He didn't let go, but he didn't try to take me down either. I wanted out of there in the worst way, but I couldn't move without hurting him. I didn't want to hurt him. I wanted to wake him up. I wanted to understand him. For him to understand me.

I wanted my father back.

After a while, his sobs died down, and he let me go and hugged himself.

I pulled the box from my pocket and plucked the card free. Sat down beside him. He turned his face away.

It took a good minute to work through the ribbon and the wrapping paper and the miles of tape. I held my breath as I tipped open the lid. The box held only one thing, a precious thing. A small sand dollar with a nick on its side. The same one from that day at the beach with Mom.

She'd had a bit of silver added to turn it into a pendant and strung a hemp cord so I could wear it if I wanted. I tied the cord around my neck. I felt Dad's eyes on my as I pulled the card from the envelope and read.

Kevin,

I know you're growing up and all. But remember I'm proud of you. Remember the magic.

Love,

Mom

I handed the card to him, waiting while he read and wiped his blotchy face with his hands.

"I'm sorry, Kevin."

An apology. Thank God. "We're gonna make it okay. Let's put some of these things back."

"It hurts to see them."

"I got that, Dad. But it hurts me not to see them. It's like they're proof she was here."

He nodded. And ripped the card in half.

"The hell?"

"You don't get to mourn her. She's not dead. If I catch you mourning her again, I'll—" He sucked in a breath.

"You'll what?"

He started to answer, then snapped his mouth shut, picked himself up, and dusted himself off. He let the pieces of the card float to the floor and marched down the attic stairs without another word.

In the silence that followed, I couldn't wrap my mind around what had just happened, what my father had just said and done. I had no one to talk to—even if I could talk to Scott, he wouldn't understand.

I wanted to feel angry. To fucking rage. Instead, I felt worry so overwhelming, I didn't think I could stand under the weight of it. But on top of that, pressing down like six tons of iron, was deep shame. That this had happened to my family. That my dad had gone off the deep end. That I would never be normal.

In the place my dad had just vacated, the King appeared.

It startled me. Snapped me from past to present.

The King had done this to me with his magic. With his immense power.

I still had no clue how to use my power. It came upon me unawares—Scott at the party. Rude at the bus. My mom's voice in the attic.

That moment—the moment I'd heard her voice in my mind—was the first time I could point to magic in my life. It was also the first time I'd heard my father talk about Mom not being dead. And therefore the first time the fae had entered my life, and I hadn't even known.

The King had brought me back to this memory for a reason. This was the point from which he intended to stamp out my memory of all things fae.

On the floor of the attic, amidst the boxes that contained all the proof of my mother's life, I met his gaze.

I understood what he meant to do, and that he had what he needed to break me first. My most private moments. The ones I'd put one foot in front of the other to survive. And what did I have?

Fear. Shame. Regret. Grief. Did fae even feel those emotions? Did they feel at all? Or were they strictly human emotions, alive in the human heart?

Human hearts. Where magic lived.

Humanity has its own magic.

CHAPTER 30

ON'T BE AFRAID TO BE VULNERABLE. Simone's words.

She'd had given me an extra shot of humanity, of her human magic. She'd poured it into me, giving it away with her whole heart, urging me—asking me to promise—that even if it scared me and even if I never wanted to be vulnerable as long as I lived, I would be willing to be willing. She'd given me the lock. The King was the key.

I pushed to my knees, leaning forward, nose-to-nose with him, never turning my eyes away. The dusty attic and stacked boxes faded from all but my peripheral vision. I brushed away the sight and feeling of the torn card and Christmas box and sand dollar.

The King's lips curved in a slight, smug grin. He thought he had me hypnotized. Only when I reached out to touch his face did that grin falter. As my fingertips made contact with his skin—his light— his eyes widened.

He'd dived into my memories, demanding and taking access to the deepest parts of me. I might not know how his magic worked, but my magic could only show me the way if I trusted it.

He'd traveled to the depths of my mind using his own. He could not demand vulnerability from me without offering it himself. No matter how hard he tried to hide it, no matter how many walls he put up.

I felt sure I would die then and there, and prayed with everything I had.

I dove into his mind.

He threw roadblocks in my path. Terrible, lethal visions to snare me. Nightmares full of blood and rent flesh and insanity.

Mom, moaning in the wreckage of her T-boned car, the left side of her body broken, lung punctured, holding onto consciousness with everything she had. Trying to hold on for me.

An earthquake of fear shook me from the inside out.

Rude paying the price for Oscar's escape from Faery, ripped to shreds just outside Simone's bus in the small hours of the morning, his soul sucked out.

A scream clawed up my throat.

Dad collapsed and dying in the Faery woods, wearing stained, holey clothes, his eyes not seeing anyone or anything.

The scream exploded from my mouth.

All I wanted was to help them. The only way to do that was to let go of the past, all the possible futures. To be right here. Right now.

I shoved forward, my mind scoring a path into the King's. Burning my way through his traps and defenses by sheer force of harnessed human will. I didn't know what I was looking for.

But I knew when I found it.

CHAPTER 31

A PEAT FIRE BURNED in the hearth, warming the room with a golden glow. Thick rugs in moss green and dark red covered the packed earth floor. Not a single chair in the place, just a groove as long as the room worn from pacing.

The only furniture was a wide stone table plastered with paper maps that bore no resemblance to anything I'd ever seen. These showed elevations instead of roads, and notches in red-marked gateways between the realm of Faery and the human world. One particular note commanded absolute attention. An X had been drawn in by hand beside a picture of a house. The King stared hard at it.

All of his careful planning came down to that place and the child that lived there. Tomorrow night, the Hunt would ride, and they would scoop up that little girl, take her back to Faery. Bring her home.

His body trembled. He willed the shaking to stop, but it refused to obey. He shouldn't be here. He should be anywhere but here.

The memory claimed him, sticking to him, refusing to let him go.

The day he'd first seen the little girl, he'd been out, wandering among the humans. Noticing the mind-numbing juxtaposition of plastic six-pack rings and empty cigarette wrappers and plastic bottles to the finely formed garden, tomatoes and squash and lettuces, their leaves gilded in the orange wash of the setting sun.

Filth and beauty. Trash and treasure. All of it glowed from the inside with the deep blue-green light of magic. Not as strongly as it should. Not even close.

He came upon a stone house with a tin roof and ambled past open windows without a soul noticing. No one ever saw him unless he wished it.

The woman inside had just put up a pot of homemade red sauce. The scent intoxicated. She hummed and sang, tried to puzzle out the lyrics to a song from her childhood and checked the clock to note the hour and a half until her husband came home.

The little girl ran from around the far corner of the house in a blur of blue and white and blond, shrieking with delight, half-tumbling over her own feet and half-bowled over by a grizzled yellow dog. She shot to her feet, the heels of her hands and the knees of her jeans and the front of her shirt grass-stained.

She looked right at him—or at where he stood. It was just a grazing glance. It didn't register anyone or anything. He thought nothing of her. Not until he took in her face.

She looked like fae daughter, made flesh and bone. Made human.

His knees buckled. He caught his balance on the side of the house. Braced himself inside and out, then closed his eyes, trying—failing— to peel away the fibers of the memory.

He spoke with the authority of thunder, the electricity of lightning, the power of a storm gathering, on the verge of unleashing its might.

Get out of my mind.

CHAPTER 32

T HE KING RAISED an electrical charge so thick and sharp, it danced along the edges of his body. He hurled a magical punch so hard it knocked the air from my lungs. But it didn't knock me from his mind. I held on too tightly. As if my life depended on it. As if all our lives did.

That's the kind of thinking that killed her, the King said.

Now we were getting somewhere.

The King punched again. This time, a headache bloomed in the back of my head. It tasted like poison. My gorge rose. I swallowed hard to keep from throwing up. Gritted my teeth.

I glimpsed a memory—a fae girl with a body of light who looked exactly like the one made of breath and skin. Not one difference between them—not a hair on her head nor a freckle on her nose. Same age, about seven. This girl, the one made of light, was fading. Literally.

She lay on a bed surrounded by the King and Queen and a bunch of other folks I took to be doctors. No one knew what to do, how to help her. She had minutes to live.

In those minutes, the Queen told her daughter over and over how much she loved her. The King held her hand and thought about how much she loved to run with the hounds, and about all the trees she'd climbed, and how she'd wandered through a gate that shouldn't have been left open, into the human world and straight into hell.

A human hell. Your people did this to her. You did this.

Seeming like any regular kid (if any human child could possibly have been that beautiful), she'd walked into the private street party of a couple of drunk men. Puddles on the concrete, sheened with motor oil. Stink of cheap Scotch. Humidity so thick, it clung to the skin. The men had set a lure. They'd been hunting.

I saw them the way the King had seen them. Dirty and wasted, with their hands on his child. The one with the black hair who played sidekick and kept his mouth shut died immediately when the King cursed him dead.

The other one, scraggly brown beard and the flannel shirt, had said, "One step further and I'll cut her throat."

He had a pure iron knife. A true threat. She wasn't just any girl to him, any prey. He knew what she was.

He wanted to hurt her.

Fear filled the pit of my belly. Watching, I could hardly breathe.

The King raised a hand. That was all. *Let's be reasonable. Let's talk. Calm down. Just lower the knife.*

He waited for some sign that the human understood him. The human was unpredictable and hungry. He had to get his girl out of there. Now.

He never got the chance.

I won't watch this happen again. I won't—

The human sliced with the blade. The girl's throat exploded in a spray of light.

The King made a fist, then snapped it open. The human exploded in a spray of blood.

After that, the King could do nothing for his daughter except bring her home. And hold her hand as she faded.

If only he'd acted a heartbeat sooner. If only he'd ignored the bastard's blade against the delicate skin of her throat. If only he'd killed the bastard.

He *had* ordered the execution of the hapless fae who'd left the gate open and unguarded. He took no pleasure in it, though it had to be done.

I felt the King reach out with his magic to stop the flood of pain. His magic broke before the onslaught as the memory replayed itself in excruciating detail.

The grain of the oak gate. The motor oil sheen on the street puddles. The scent of brine from Galveston Bay, overpowered by the whisky, but there nonetheless.

I was the girl, trapped and confused and terrified. The realization that I'd made a mistake so profound I would never get a chance to apologize flowed through me like a wash of tears. I'd never get to live. The last thing I'd see was the fear and cold fury on my father's face.

I felt the King tremble.

I was the captor, who lived on the edge of the civilized city, infected and mesmerized by magic, believing that if I could only capture some for myself, the world would make sense again. Would stop tearing me up inside. Stop throwing me away like yesterday's trash.

I felt the King's heart constrict, a spasm of longing and sorrow.

I was the King, with all the power of an entire world running in my veins. I couldn't save the one person who meant everything to me. I could only watch her die. No revenge slaked the black hole in my heart.

I felt the King's eyes well with unshed tears. A thousand years' worth. An unbearable weight.

He let the weight fall. His sobs trembled the ground beneath my feet. Shook the heavens above with thunder. Scored the sky with lightning. Tears poured, washing away the dust that had covered the memories for so long, making it all clean. Shiny. Raw.

The power of it took my breath away.

When the King's tears finally ebbed, I asked the question that hovered at the edges of my heart.

What was her name?

CHAPTER 33

I KNEW BETTER than to ask, but if the girl had been human, I would have wanted to know. To remember her.

The King didn't speak, but I read her name in his thoughts: Brook, no E.

Brook, like the stream she'd liked to swim in when she was small. A thousand years ago. If he allowed himself to experience the full brute force of his grief, if he opened to it at all, he would cease to exist.

"Did you take the human girl who looked like her?" I asked aloud.

He met my gaze, eyes filled with tears. "Yes."

"What happened to her?"

"She wept for her parents. For her human life. She grew old and she died. She never loved."

A massive wave of grief and loss dragged through me. I gasped and fought for air. Drowning. I swiped a hand over my wet face, and felt that other stolen life.

"And Simone?"

He blanched, the truth of what she was to him written all over his face.

My voice rose with every word. "Is that all you are? Someone who does terrible things? Is that what you want?"

"It can't be undone."

No, it couldn't. Nothing would ever make it right, not for any of them. Not for any of us.

Fury reignited in my heart. "You don't have to keep doing it! You don't have to hurt the ones who come too close. You don't have to be the terror."

He shook his head. "Those with ill intent—"

My throat wanted to close. I held on to breath with every ounce of will. "They could be hurting, just like you."

His voice cracked. "You can't possibly know—"

Magic cracked through me like a whip. "I care. Why the fuck don't you?"

He held my gaze. Took a step back because of what he saw there.

"Enough," he said. "If you expect me to see the world differently—"

"To *be* different."

"I can't change," he said.

He expected me to change, but he wouldn't even try. He'd ruined my life because he feared me, because I was dangerous to him. He wouldn't kill me because I was somehow important to the Faery Realm's survival. He would fight forever.

I would fight forever.

He stared at me. "How do you know those things about the realm? About me?"

He'd read them in my mind, so he knew how. Simone had told me.

"Do you know how you're important to Faery?" he asked.

I blinked at him. "You don't know?"

"It's the one thing I don't."

"That makes two of us."

He looked me up and down. "You're not going to stop, are you?"

"Fighting for the people I love? No."

"It's more than that. You're more than that."

I didn't know whether I believed that. It didn't matter. Right now, I was just me, and that was enough. I was enough.

"If you expect me to allow my world to be connected with the human world, to respect your world and the people who live in it, I need something from you."

I narrowed my eyes. "What?"

"A connection. Someone who can bridge both worlds. Who can see and speak to both humans and fae."

I'd never wanted anything like that. All I'd been able to think about at first was how to get back to my own screwed-up version of normal, and that had been overpowered by the need to save my dad. My friends. Simone.

If I could keep terrible things from happening to someone else, shouldn't I?

"How can I trust you?"

"I'll be trusting you just as much," he said.

"We leave here. All of us. And you fix my dad first."

"Agreed," the King said. "You have my word."

A fae's word was their bond. "Simone, too."

He shook his head. "It's too late for her. She's lost."

Some things couldn't be undone. It wasn't right. It wasn't fair. But it was true.

"Do we have a deal, Kevin?"

I listened, allowing my magic the space and time to rise, to tell me whether this was the right thing to do. But that wasn't how it worked. It warned of danger. It gave me a chance to correct course. To choose love. To choose life.

I heard nothing at all.

In the blessed silence, I spoke the single word that would seal all our fates.

"Yes."

CHAPTER 34

W E RETURNED to the human world on the bus, arriving a few minutes before dawn. Nothing had ever felt as good as descending the steps and setting foot on the solid asphalt, or hearing the rumble of engines and wheels on concrete that drifted the few blocks from the freeway. Nothing felt as amazing as wrapping my arms around each of my friends in turn, the terror of the last few days broken like a fever. Even the October chill had shifted, the wind turning to blow from the southeast, drawing brine and humidity from the Gulf.

The Explorer was right where I'd left it, parked at the mouth of the alley. I walked Dad over, finally relaxing when he leaned against passenger door, looking as wrung out as I felt, eyes clear and sober. The scary wildness was gone. He seemed like his whole self again.

"Never thought I'd see this place again," he said.

I agreed. "Same goes."

"Are we okay, Kevin?"

We had so much to talk about, a lot to work through, AA meetings to attend. There were no guarantees, but we had a chance. Before, I'd have given anything for that, and now it was here.

"I think we will be."

Dad sighed, his relief a palpable thing.

I glanced over my shoulder at Amy, Rude, Scott, and Oscar still huddled near the bus. "I need to—"

"I know. Go ahead."

I turned at the same time they moved to meet me halfway. Oscar nodded to me as we met, then kept walking toward the car.

"He okay?" I asked.

"Yeah." Rude ran a hand over his buzz cut. "I have no idea how. We should all be toast. Dude, you're gonna have to tell me how you did that."

"Not any time soon, man."

He cracked a half smile. "You can wait 'til tomorrow."

Funny man. Class clown. Magical motherfucker.

Scott shoved his hands into his jeans pockets. He had hollows beneath his eyes, his color not quite what it ought to be. "If it's all the same to you, I'd rather not know."

"You probably need to," Rude said.

"I need, like, a month. At least a month. And I don't want to see any of you until then."

"It's too much?" I asked.

"No," he said. "It's just different, hearing you talk about it and, you know, experiencing."

Amy nodded. "Truth."

I met her gaze. "Are you all right?"

She didn't answer for a moment. "I was so worried."

"Me, too," I said.

She closed the distance between us and hugged me as if she never wanted to let go, whispering in my ear. "Can we start over?"

I wanted that. I wanted second chances. I wanted something good.

"What day is it?" Scott asked.

Rude answered. "Saturday, I think."

"One day off and then we have to go back to school. Sucks."

Rude laughed. Amy turned in my arms, joining in.

I looked at them, then over at the car, where Oscar talked with

Dad. They'd saved me long before I returned the favor, and for that I'd be forever grateful. But I hadn't been able to save everyone.

Not yet.

The first light of dawn brightened the horizon, gold and lavender and full of promise. At the end of the alley, the yellow school bus shimmered, twinkle lights in its windows flashing, before it faded slowly from sight.

Simone had kept her promise to me. I'd keep mine to her if it was the last thing I did. Everything had changed. We'd changed. Whatever we might have been—might still be—to each other didn't matter. What mattered was that she lived.

She was in Faery, somewhere, humanity gone. She was alone, but not lost, because I wouldn't stop until she was found. Hope was a real thing, just like magic, as real as breath, as real as a heartbeat.

I didn't have to trust in that. I didn't have to believe.

I knew.

If you enjoyed this book, please consider leaving a review. It doesn't have to be long—even a few words will be very appreciated.

Reviews make it possible for an author to continue writing books in a series. They make a big difference in helping to get the word out about a book or a series. And reviews can make the all difference in the world when a reader wants to take a chance on a new author, but isn't sure whether they will like the book.

Thank you for taking hours out of your busy life to read. I hope this book brought you time to escape into a story, and that it brought you joy.

Turn the page to read Chapter 1 of the next book in *The Faery Chronicles*, **Faery Prophet**.

FAERY PROPHET - CHAPTER 1

STICKY SEPTEMBER SATURDAY NIGHT in Houston, Texas, on a sidewalk outside of The Rollins Pub, where Johnny Rocket played his thunder bass. People in various stages of inebriation mingled and the stink of stale beer lingered. Not the normal hangout spot for a sober dude without a fake ID. But, hey, I had responsibilities and a mostly secret identity.

My name? Rudolph Diamond Davies III. Rude, to my friends. Unofficially, the class clown. The party guy. The one with the uncanny luck. Always ready to be a friend or help out a dude in need. My official assignment: Save life. Prevent death. And other bad things.

I leaned against the brick wall outside the pub and stared at the old oak on the other side of the walk. Anyone else would see an ordinary tree whose ordinary roots buckled the sidewalk—if they noticed it at all. Me? I saw a portal to and from the Otherworld.

Otherworld, as in the place where faeries, demons, and angels lived. Sometimes they traveled through portals, aka gates, into the human realm. Sometimes they even came with good intentions.

I had it on good authority, however, that a visitor planned to bust through tonight bleeding bad vibes and looking for trouble. As the youngest (and only) faery seer apprentice to the (only) full seer in town, I'd use my magic to turn them around. Send them back.

I kept my gaze on the tree. Didn't even blink. Until I spotted a girl I knew from senior English out of the corner of my eye.

Melody. Pretty name for a cheerleader-next-door kind of girl. Wavy blond hair brushed her shoulders. Her blue eyes sparkled when she saw me. I didn't know what to do except smile. And stare.

She didn't look like herself.

She wore red stilettos so tall and sharp, they practically sparked on the pavement. A short black skirt swung high on her thighs and a white tank hugged her every considerable curve. Definitely different clothes than she wore Monday through Friday.

Her cheekbones seemed a little high and sharp. Her mouth looked more severe. A worry line had erupted in the center of her forehead.

It wasn't just the clothes and the changes in her face that bothered me, though. She had a halo around her body the color of mud. What psychics would call a bad aura. A portent of violence—against herself or someone else? Either way, worry-making.

She pulled a pack of smokes from a tiny black purse and lit one as she sidled up to me. She elbowed me in the ribs, trying to be playful and failing—because that worry line? It didn't go away.

"Hey, Rude," she said in her husky voice.

"Hey, yourself. Didn't think I'd see you here."

"Same goes. What are you up to?"

"Holding up the wall," I said. Not exactly a lie. "Too bad I can't get in. Johnny Rocket's sounding real good. What I can hear of him, anyway."

She laughed. The line in her brow stayed through that, too. "How is it that a guy who throws the best keg parties in town—parties that practically the entire school comes to—doesn't have an ID for some-place like this?"

"I plead innocence."

"You?"

"Yeah, me. Really. You feeling okay?"

"Do I look like I have a fever or something?" She leaned in close, I guess so I could feel her forehead and give my best non-MD opinion. So close I could smell her subtle amber perfume. And underneath it, something stranger.

A sickly sweet scent, like cough syrup. And sulfur.

I took a deep breath to be sure and blew it out slow.

"Well?" she asked.

"You seem like you're in trouble." I thought twice about saying the second thing, but the way she looked? And the smell? I had to know, and the best way to do that was to use the element of vocal surprise. Best case scenario, she'd just think I was weird. I was okay with that. Worst case? I hoped we didn't go there.

So I said, "And you smell like a demon."

Her eyes narrowed. "That's not nice."

I hadn't meant it to be, exactly. I held her gaze.

She fidgeted under my über-scrutiny.

"I repeat: trouble. What's up, Melody? I can help."

"No faery seer apprentice can help me," she said. But not convincingly. Spoken like somebody fishing for confirmation or information.

I'd wanted her to spill her guts about the problem. Or if something had possessed her (hey, it happened), it might un-possess her and run. I hadn't expected her to spout off about my extracurricular activities. One, because she shouldn't have known. Two, because she shouldn't have known.

My turn to fidget. "Will you tell me what you mean by that?"

She took a drag on her smoke. Her fingers trembled. "I have a confession. I didn't come here to see Johnny Rocket. I came to see you."

"How?"

"I took the bus."

"No," I said. "How did you know where to find me?"

"I've been having some seriously screwed-up feelings lately. I'm angry all the time."

"You have a lot to be pissed off about."

She held my gaze. "You, too?"

"Look, people talk. You know that. I heard some stuff at school."

"From?"

"It's not important, Melody."

"The hell it's not. Probably those girls pretending to be my *friends*." She raised her hands and made air quotes for emphasis.

I nodded. One person's private tragedy could become another person's juicy gossip. In Melody's case, the gossip went like this: Her stepfather beat the crap out of her. She showed up at school with a sunrise of bruises and two black eyes about a month ago. She left home. Went to stay with Beth Barrett, everyone's favorite science fiction geek, for a couple of days that turned into a more permanent arrangement.

The stepdad had been arrested and then let go because neither Melody's mom nor Melody pressed charges. Mom loved him more than she loved her own daughter. And he terrified Melody.

Although the people at school talked about all this like it'd been a one-time thing, I had my doubts.

"Those girls who started the rumors are assholes," I said.

"Thanks," she said. "This anger thing? It's not about him. It's not even about my…mother. It's like power surges or something. I can't control when it happens. I can barely keep from punching my fist through the wall. And I know stuff. It just pops into my head. Like what you are. And where to find you—like I could…"

"What?"

She hesitated. "Smell you. From all the way across town."

"The only people I know who can do that aren't human. But you are."

"Not entirely."

I blinked at her.

She flushed. "I know it sounds crazy."

"No."

"Maybe not to you. You're a freak who hangs out with other freaks." She sucked in a breath. "No offense."

I tried not to take any. After all, it was kind of accurate. "So if you're not one-hundred-percent human, what else are you?"

The words tumbled out fast and low, for my ears only. "Demon, I think. Like you said."

I couldn't think of a worse thing. Not one. "How?"

"I found some stuff in my mom's diary. Stuff about my real dad. I was looking for money, you know? Sometimes she hides bills in there. I mean, she hasn't written anything in it for years, but she still keeps it. And it says outright that my actual dad wasn't human. That she had suspicions when she met him, but she didn't find out for sure until after I was born. She said my eyes were red, Rude. They turned blue, the way other kids' eyes start out blue and turn brown."

I studied her face. She didn't seem to be making up any of this. She spoke the dead-on truth as she understood it. "Woah."

"Exactly. What do I do?"

I had no idea how to answer that question. I'd heard of human and Otherworld hybrids before, but I'd never seen one. I'd certainly never met one. If I found out something like that about myself, I'd be terrified of what I might do to other people. Non-humans…well, they weren't *human*. They didn't think the same way. They didn't have the same kinds of morals. They did *bad* things.

I swallowed hard. "Did you ask your mom about it?"

"You're kidding, right?" She peered at my not-kidding face. "Okay, I kind of did. I said *so this is a joke* and she stared at me. So I said *this is like a metaphor* and she looked away from me. I said *this is real?* and she told me to get out. That was the last thing that happened before I left home."

"After your stepfather hit you."

She winced.

"Sorry. When was the last time you had an anger flash?"

"Two nights ago."

"Anything weird happen?"

"I destroyed my trash can. You know, in my room."

"Define *destroyed*."

"One second it was normal and the next it, like, melted. I completely lost my mind. I spent the rest of the night curled up in a ball in the closet."

Holy crap. "You ever done anything like that before?"

"Two weeks ago. To the steering wheel of my car. Well, Beth's car. Her mom was so beyond mad. Which is why I took the bus."

"How many times has it happened total?" I asked.

"Twelve."

"And you didn't come to me until now?"

Her voice started out low and rose with each word. "I would've if I'd known about you before this afternoon."

Her complexion took on a red cast. This time, she didn't look embarrassed. Frustrated, maybe. Frustrated could lead to mad, which I didn't want to see. Not yet, anyway. I held up both hands to signal a truce.

She looked away. Cocked her head. "What's that?"

The bark of the oak tree had begun to shimmer. The Otherworld gate had been activated. Another thing humans couldn't usually see.

I put out my arm. Pushed her behind me.

"What?" she asked again.

"It could be dangerous," I said.

"So could I."

Well, yeah. But I had to choose my battles.

A bang and crunch behind us had me throwing a desperate glance over my shoulder. Just a couple of bouncers setting down and flipping open a chest filled with bottled water and ice.

I faced front again. A small horde of grackles had landed in the branches of the tree, and the gate within the trunk had stopped shimmering and started to pulse. The brown of the bark brightened until it bled white. All the hair on my body stood straight up. Luckily, I had a buzz cut or I'd have looked like Einstein, only with orange hair.

"Jesus, Rude!" Melody whisper-shouted in my ear.

"Welcome to my world."

Just Melody and me and whoever traveled through the tree. No one else could see. They talked and laughed. Lit smokes and, from the smell, joints. They flirted as if the world around them was safe.

The tree groaned. Split wide open to reveal a pair of thick, black lace-ups. Attached to two stocky legs in black pants. The being also wore a belt with a flashlight, a radio, and a gun. A cop's blue shirt, silver badge and all—official HPD wear. His arms came through next, brown and brushed with fine, black hair. I marked the pinky ring on his finger and knew him before I saw his face and met his watchful gaze.

"Officer Burns," I said.

He looked me up and down. Curled his lip as if he found Hawaiian shirts and cargo shorts and sneakers distasteful. "Rudolph Diamond Davies."

"That's 'Mr. Davies' to you."

Melody took hold of my shirt. Shook it to get my attention. "A cop?"

"No, he's just dressed like one. He's faery."

"An imposter faery cop?"

"Chill. I'll handle him."

Or *them*. Because where Burns went, his evil twin, Officer Reid, always followed.

Sure enough, Burns stepped away from the gate. Two seconds later, redheaded, freckled Reid stepped through the tree's gate and onto the sidewalk, beer gut hung over his belt. He got in my face, nose-to-nose.

"We heard something bad's getting ready to go down," he said. "If you know anything, Davies, you'd better spill it now."

I shoved my index finger into his chest. "I heard you were the bad thing."

He ignored that. "The King sent us. He's concerned."

Didn't he always? Wasn't he always? At least, the one and only time I'd met these busters before, the Faery King had ordered them to make my best friend's life a living hell. Kevin had been Joe-normal before they came on the scene. After a whole lot of imminent mortal danger, he'd ended up a go-between. A liaison between the human and faery races.

"Why didn't you contact Kev?" I asked.

"That was our intention. We were to go from here to his home. But you're here, so we're asking you and you're going to tell us."

"Or what? Arrogant much?"

Reid thinned his lips. His hands curled into fists.

Burns laid a hand on his partner's shoulder. Reid seethed, but he backpedaled two steps. Out of my immediate space.

"The King wouldn't have sent us if it weren't important," Burns said. "All the signs in our realm point to something terrible about to happen. We know it begins here. That's all we know."

His words faded into silence. Like, actual silence. Although the crowd outside the pub never noticed the gate or anyone walking out of it, they sure noticed the sudden appearance of two officers of the law. I glanced over my shoulder. Caught sight of two dudes walking away from us fast. Probably the guys with the pot. Everybody else resumed talking, only lower-key than before.

I felt hot. Hotter than usual for a September night. I wiped away trickles of sweat headed for my eyes and focused on Burns again. "I have no idea what you're talking about."

He moved in front of Reid and spoke low. "What about your master? Did he say anything to you?"

I bristled at *master*. I had a teacher. Oscar. Owner of a damned good Tex-Mex restaurant by day, faery seer by night. "Just that some troublemaker would be coming through the gate tonight."

He brushed his hair back from his forehead with both hands. "Nothing else?"

The way he looked and the desperate-hopeful way he asked the question had me pulling my cell from the front pocket of my shorts and dialing right away. I tried Oscar's land line first. Six rings and voicemail. Same with the cell. Not unusual for him to be out. He could be on a mission like I was. Or at the club with his boyfriend, Harvard.

I texted him. Wiped my eyes again.

Melody tugged on my shirt again. "Rude? What's going on?"

I glanced over my shoulder. "No idea, but I'm gonna figure it out. And, hey, don't worry about these two. They're not here for you."

"It's not them," she said. "I don't feel right."

Officer Burns sidestepped into my line of sight. "We need your full attention, Davies."

"Just a minute," I said.

I turned on my heel and got a full-on gander at Melody. She had that frustrated, red look that'd made me nervous before the King's faux officers showed up. Also, a wave of heat flowed off of her. More sweat beaded at my hairline.

My heart thumped in my chest. "Is this how it felt before? When you melted the trash can and the steering wheel?"

She nodded.

"Calm down. Deep breaths." I took one and blew it out in a rush.

She followed my example. Once. Twice. Three times. It didn't cool the heat. Her aura took on a distinctly fire-and-smoke color.

Reid paled behind him. "Look at her."

"Holy Mother," Burns said.

She was burning up. She'd go nuclear any second. Melt something. Or someone. If she didn't cool down. If—

I bolted for the ice chest. Shouldered the couple of people standing around it out of the way. Wrestled it off the ground and ran back toward Melody and the faery cops.

I heaved the ice at Melody. It rained over her in a fall of white, and most of it shattered and scattered on the concrete like pebbles. The rest hung in her hair and stuck to her clothes. Slid down her skin in melted streams that turned to steam.

Steam.

Now people stared at us. At her. One girl's laugh rose above every other noise, then cut off.

Melody pressed her hands against her eyes. Turned away.

I caught sight of something strange on her back. Something her tank top didn't cover. Black and grey on her skin. A tattoo. Since when did Melody have ink?

Since when did Melody have ink that writhed like snakes?

I took a step toward her. "Melody, look at me."

She shook her head. "It's not working."

"What's that on your back?" I asked.

She didn't answer. The heat streaming from her rose like waves rose from asphalt at high noon in August. Meltdown imminent.

Burns saw it, too. He pulled back his arm and punched her in the side of the head. Any human girl would've lost consciousness. Ended up on the ground, probably with a concussion.

Not Melody. She turned on Burns, face screwed up in fury, and kneed him in the balls. He clutched his crotch and went down.

If ice didn't work and she couldn't be knocked out, that left magic. I could banish an Otherworld being back to its own world, but she was part human. She belonged here.

I could blunt powers. I couldn't counteract them all the way, just enough to keep them from working one hundred percent. It'd saved my life more than once. I'd ended up scarred instead of dead.

I closed my eyes. Found the still place inside my belly where my magic lived. It pooled there like water, cool and dark and deep. Shone like a light illuminated it from the inside.

I breathed it up. It rose along my spine with every inhale. Until it got to my shoulders—then it rolled along my arms into my hands. I lifted them. Pointed them toward Melody.

"Something's happening," she said.

Officer Reid looked at her. At me. He saw what I was doing. Frowned. Moved out of range of my hands. Burns crawled away.

Melody's eyes widened. "Rude. Oh, God."

"I'm trying something."

"Try faster."

The magic flowed from the center of my palms in a wash of watery light. It spilled over her, head to toe.

She shrieked. Curled in on herself.

The slap of flip-flops and a girl's voice sounded behind me. "Hey, jerk—leave her alone."

I couldn't afford to break eye contact with Melody to look at her. I knew she couldn't see the magic. Only Melody in pain. "I'm not touching her."

"She's hurting just the same."

"I'm helping her."

"You're creeping her out. You're creeping me out."

"She's under the influence," I said. "Not sure what she took, okay?"

"That's why she attacked the cops?" the girl asked.

I nodded.

Not that the cops were behaving like cops who'd been attacked. They ought to be taking her to the ground. Or overreacting with a Taser. Anything but what they'd done.

Melody met my gaze. "Rude?"

"Yeah?"

"I'm sorry."

I didn't get a chance to ask what for. She blinked. Her eyes turned from blue to red and back again.

A wave of nausea started in the soles of my feet and sped up my legs and gut and chest and throat and head before I could take another breath. The beating of my heart became a roar of blood that filled my ears. Until the girl behind me screamed. She screamed and screamed until I thought my head would explode.

I rushed to Melody. Wrapped her in my arms. Put myself between her and everyone else. Hoped to God that if she hurt anyone, it would be me. No one else.

I held on with all I had. Her heat poured into me. Ripped the air from my lungs. I gasped for breath. Couldn't speak a word.

My knees turned to rubber. My body tipped to the left. I couldn't balance. I refused to let her go. She fell with me.

The sidewalk rushed up to meet us.

ALSO BY LESLIE CLAIRE WALKER

THE AWAKENED MAGIC SAGA

THE SOUL FORGE

(The Complete Series)

Angel Hunts

Angel Rises

Angel Falls

Angel Strikes

Angel Roars

Angel Burns

THE FAERY CHRONICLES

(The Complete Series)

Faery Novice

Faery Prophet

Faery Sovereign

SHORT STORY COLLECTIONS

Ink & Blood

Ink & Stars

Ink & Sword

ACKNOWLEDGMENTS

All my thanks and love to T. Thorn Coyle and Jo Anne Banker for helping to make this book the best it could be.

ABOUT THE AUTHOR

Since the age of seven, Leslie Claire Walker has wanted to be Princess Leia—wise and brave and never afraid of a fight, no matter the odds.

Leslie hails from the concrete and steel canyons and lush bayous of southeast Texas—a long way from Alderaan. Now, she lives in the rain-drenched Pacific Northwest with a cast of spectacular characters, including cats, harps, fantastic pieces of art that may or may not be doorways to other realms, and too many fantasy novels to count.

She is the author of **The Faery Chronicles** and **Soul Forge** series, two complete series of urban fantasy novels, novellas, and stories filled with found family, angels, assassins, faeries, and demons.

Connect with Leslie
leslieclairewalker.com
leslie@leslieclairewalker.com

COPYRIGHT INFORMATION

FAERY NOVICE
Copyright © 2018 Leslie Claire Walker
Published 2018 by Secret Fire Press
Cover and Layout Copyright © 2018 by Secret Fire Press
Cover Design by Lou Harper
Cover Art Copyright © Lou Harper

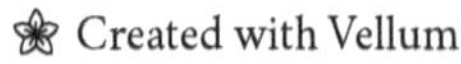 Created with Vellum